SHERRYL WOODS has published over forty novels since 1982 and has sold over four million books worldwide. She has written six Amanda Roberts mysteries and she received the *Romantic Times* award for Best New Author of Romantic Suspense of 1988. A former real-life news reporter in the South, very much like her highly praised fictional sleuth Amanda Roberts, Sherryl Woods now lives in Key Biscayne, Florida.

Sherryl Woods

Hide and Seek

WARNER BOOKS

A Time Warner Company

WARNER BOOKS EDITION

Cover design by Jackie Merri Meyer
Cover photo by Herman Estevez

Warner Books, Inc.
1271 Avenue of the Americas
New York, NY 10020

 A Time Warner Company

Printed in the United States of America

First Printing: December, 1993

10 9 8 7 6 5 4 3 2 1

CHAPTER

One

*T*HE thing Amanda Roberts liked most about her
newly rented house in the Virginia-Highland area
of Atlanta was the relatively close access to Piedmont Park, a glorious stretch of grass edged by flowers
and shaded by towering old trees, filled with picnic pavil-
ions, softball diamonds, and tennis courts, and home to
the Atlanta Botanical Gardens. Once a year the park also
played host to an arts festival. It wasn't her beloved Cen-
tral Park in Manhattan, but it was close.

The thing she hated most about her new house was its
proximity to that very same park's jogging paths. Everyone seemed to think she ought to be using them. Her research assistant, Jenny Lee Macon, had made a practice of
coming home from work with her three nights a week just
to see to it that Amanda ran—or more precisely limped—
through that damned park. Amanda had tried explaining
that fitness training was not part of Jenny Lee's job description, but so far her arguments had fallen on deaf ears.

And, on the days she chose to be entirely honest with

herself, Amanda had to admit that she felt better. Only marginally, perhaps, but better just the same. She would not have conceded the fact to Jenny Lee, however, even if she'd been taken out and tortured.

Nor, she decided as she laced up her jogging shoes, would she ever tell her that she'd actually run on her own on a night when Jenny Lee had gone off on a date with photographer Larry Carter and left Amanda to her own devices. A Tuesday, no less. An off night.

Dear Lord, she hoped she wasn't becoming addicted to exercise at this late stage in her life. She quickly popped an entire handful of chocolate-pudding-and-toasted marshmallow jelly beans into her mouth just to prove that she hadn't entirely turned her back on sugar. She vowed to eat a huge steak tonight, too. Maybe a hot-fudge sundae. It wouldn't do to get too healthy. She was almost certain it went against some journalistic code. Since she didn't smoke and rarely drank beer, sugar was her only vice.

The park was teeming with runners, bikers, and folks out for a brisk walk on the chilly spring night. She spent a dutiful ten minutes doing her stretching exercises—what she could remember of them—then set off at a clip that wouldn't exactly be a threat to an Olympic competitor. She smiled and waved to half a dozen people she recognized from other nights. There was something comforting about feeling as if she were already a part of her new neighborhood. After a couple of years in the boondocks outside Atlanta, it felt good to be back in a city, surrounded by activity slightly more exciting than listening to roosters crowing at dawn.

As she ran her mind miraculously cleared, quite possibly because she couldn't concentrate on anything except catching her breath. When she'd completed the mile-long route she and Jenny Lee usually covered, she felt so good she decided to push for one more mile.

It didn't take long for her to regret the decision. Her legs began to feel like lead after the first quarter mile. Then she got a stitch in her side that hobbled her. Wheezing in ragged gasps, she stopped beside the path and bent over, trying to catch her breath.

"Are you okay?" a softly accented voice asked with concern.

Amanda looked up at the woman who'd stopped to check on her. With a thin, athletic build, eyes the color of a vivid blue sky, and skin that had been turned a tawny gold by the sun, she looked vibrantly healthy. Her sweat-dampened hair, long and professionally highlighted, was caught up in a ponytail, a severe style that would have been devastating on anyone whose features weren't as perfect as this woman's. She looked to be in her late twenties, thirty at the outside. A maturing beauty queen in tank top and sneakers.

"More or less," Amanda told her with a wry grimace. "I got overly ambitious and tried to push myself."

The woman smiled sympathetically, still jogging in place. "I could wait and run with you, just to be sure you make it back okay."

"No, really. Thanks, but I'd just slow you down. You look as if you train for marathons."

"As a matter of fact, I do. It relieves the stress. It also

allows me to eat anything I want to," she admitted with a rueful expression. "I'd hate to give up cheesecake."

Amanda couldn't recall the last time she had allowed herself to indulge in cheesecake. A thick, decadent wedge of creamy New York cheesecake. The kind served in her favorite deli on Broadway. Her mouth watered.

"Exactly how far do you have to run to do that?" she inquired somewhat wistfully.

"I am for six to ten miles at least three or four times a week."

Amanda groaned. "I guess I'll stick to nonfat frozen yogurt."

The other woman laughed. "You sure you don't want me to wait for you? It's not a problem."

"No, really. I'll be fine," she said. "The pain in my side is going and I can almost breathe normally again. I'll just walk back from here."

"See you, then. Take it easy."

" 'Bye."

Envious, Amanda watched her move off. Her long stride seemed effortless. Convinced she could emulate the style with a little practice, she actually tried to mimic it for another hundred yards before conceding that she'd had it for the night. Besides, the sun was sinking rapidly, and she had no desire to be stranded on the far side of the park after nightfall. The lighting was adequate in most areas, but there were still sections she'd rather avoid once the crowds dispersed.

Amanda took a shortcut back to her starting point, then walked slowly back home. She was relieved when she was finally inside, showered, and sitting down to a huge salad she'd brought home from the produce section in the grocery store. She felt incredibly noble as she poured fat-free dressing onto the lettuce. She promised herself she'd have that less healthy steak tomorrow night.

Just after eleven, when she'd settled in bed with a book she'd been trying for the last month to find time to read, the phone rang.

"Amanda, honey, is that you?" Jenny Lee asked worriedly.

"Who else were you expecting? You called my number."

"Were you watching the news?"

"No, why?" she said, instantly alerted by Jenny Lee's tone.

"Another woman's missing," she said. "She disappeared tonight, and right from the park where we've been running. I was so worried you might have been over there. I mean, I know how you claim to hate jogging, but you get so compulsive about things, I was afraid you'd sneak in a workout and not tell me."

Amanda decided to ignore the observation about her compulsive nature. "Actually, I was over there," she admitted, her adrenaline pumping.

This was the sixth woman who had disappeared over the last year and a half. All of the first five had been young. All were professionals. All had been beautiful. All had been found, strangled. Beyond that, however, not a single link had been discovered. The police were baffled, and women all over the city were panicking, especially since the latest disappearances had come only weeks apart, suggesting that if a serial killer was, in fact, involved, he was becoming bolder and more desperate.

"What did they say on the news? Have they found her?"

"Not yet. They're searching the park. A friend reported her missing when she didn't come home from her run, but the police won't release an ID until they notify her family. It gave me the creeps listening to them, though. Do you think it's related to all those others?"

"Possibly."

"Amanda, do you think maybe we ought to investigate this for *Inside Atlanta?* Maybe profile these women or something?"

"I was just thinking the same thing."

Amanda got out of bed immediately after she hung up the phone and walked from room to room, checking the locks on the windows and doors. Back in her bedroom, she even searched the closet until she found the gun she'd had ever since an unhappy subject of one of her exposés in New York had targeted her for bomb threats and other misfortunes. So far, she'd never had to use it. She prayed almost daily that she would never have to. Given her vocal antigun stance, she felt surprisingly better once it was tucked away in her bedside nightstand. It was the first time she'd felt the need to have it nearby since she'd left New York.

Not five minutes later the phone rang again.

"Amanda?" Joe Donelli's voice sounded almost as anxious as Jenny Lee's. It was also tinged with an awareness that despite the recent improvement in their on-again, off-again relationship, the ex-cop still had no official claims on her, including no right to worry openly about her.

"Hi. Yes, I know about the disappearance. Yes, I was in the park tonight. Yes, I'm fine. Yes, the house is locked up tight."

"Okay. Okay. You can't blame a guy for worrying."

"No, I suppose not. How are you? Did you get the fields planted today?" she asked, even though it killed her to feign an interest in Donelli's farming. She still thought he ought to be out investigating, like the detective he had once excelled at being. He had his investigator's license in Georgia, but used it far too rarely in her opinion.

"Corn's in. The tomatoes will be in tomorrow. I'll probably do the beans the day after."

He sounded so damned pleased, she wanted to drive out to the country and shake him. "Joe, do you think this disappearance is related to the others?"

"The cops don't even know if the first five are linked."

"Maybe not officially, but what does your gut instinct tell you?"

"They're linked."

"I was thinking of looking into this, maybe profiling the women."

"Why doesn't that surprise me?"

She waited for his objection. He remained silent. "No lectures?" she asked, astonished.

"Not from me. I learned long ago I can't stop you from doing something once you've set your mind on it."

She sighed and hugged the phone a little tighter, grateful that they had reached an understanding about her work at long last. "Thank you."

"Don't thank me. I'll still worry." He sighed. "I'll talk to you in the morning, okay?"

"Okay. 'Night, Joe."

"Good night, darlin'."

Smiling at the hint of southern dialect mellowing his native Brooklyn accent, Amanda hung up and then drifted off to sleep.

First thing in the morning, anxious to get to work and map out a plan with Jenny Lee and Oscar, the magazine's editor, she grabbed the paper and took off for the *Inside Atlanta* offices. Only when she was at her desk, coffee cup in hand, did she spread open the *Constitution*. They had found the body in the park.

A sense of horror and unreality slammed through her as she stared at the front page. MURDERED WOMAN KILLED DURING RUN declared the four-column headline. But that was no surprise. What made Amanda's stomach churn and sent a cold chill down her spine was the woman's photograph. Even in black and white and smudged, there was no mistaking that gorgeous, delicate face, that mane of golden-streaked hair.

Lynette Rogers. Twenty-eight. A former Miss Georgia contender. A stockbroker. A marathon runner.

And the woman who'd taken time out to offer assistance to Amanda, perhaps only minutes before she had vanished.

CHAPTER

Two

*S*IX women dead, all at an age Amanda could identify with. Six women whose lives had not touched in any way the police had been able to identify. But Amanda knew with everything in her that the unsolved murders were tied together.

Though her investigative stories had been focused more on political corruption than serial murders, she'd been well acquainted with some of the best crime reporters in the country. She'd spent countless hours talking to them about the psychological profiles of serial killers, about tiny shreds of evidence that eventually did them in no matter how long it seemed that they'd committed perfect crimes. She'd read in depth about Ted Bundy and others like him, but she'd never been inclined to cover such killings herself. Spending weeks on end mired in the gruesome details, trying to follow the convoluted thoughts of someone who was mentally deranged, rather than simply greedy, struck her as an emotionally draining task.

Now, though, she found herself not just intrigued with a

complex, potentially explosive story, but angry because a woman who had stopped to help her in the park had likely fallen victim to a killer only a short time later. Meeting Lynette Rogers made the story personal in a way it might otherwise not have been. She was involved in the disappearances, whether she wanted to be or not.

She was still shaken when *Inside Atlanta* editor Oscar Cates strolled over to her desk, his face set in an expression she'd learned to distrust.

"Oh, no," she said, holding up her hands in a defensive gesture.

Oscar looked hurt. "You don't even know what I want yet."

"I know you have an assignment in mind and it's going to be one I'll hate."

"I thought you were too down-to-earth to buy into all that psychic mumbo jumbo," he retorted.

"I am."

"Then how could you possibly know what I've got in mind or how you'll feel about it?"

"Because right now, anything other than the story I'm thinking about will be one I'll hate."

Oscar dragged over a chair, sat down, and leaned toward her. She recognized the posture. He was about to resort to his sneakiest techniques of persuasion. Amanda steeled herself.

"But this is good," he said. "I was thinking maybe we ought to take a look at what's happening with the Olympics' construction. It's about time to see if it's on schedule, who's been awarded contracts, that sort of thing. Who knows? Maybe you'll dig up some scandal, improper building inspections, shoddy workmanship."

He waited expectantly for her to express fascination. When she showed no reaction, he trotted out several more possibilities that might have intrigued her on any other morning.

She shook her head. "Assign Jack Davis to do that," she said, referring to their aggressive, talented business reporter.

Oscar's gaze narrowed suspiciously. "You saying you don't want to go snooping around looking for shenanigans by public officials?"

"I want to look for a murderer."

Oscar was shaking his head before the words were out of her mouth. "Not a good idea."

"Why not? The police aren't having much luck."

It was a conversation they'd had all too frequently. Oscar was inclined to think that police were better at discovering killers because they carried guns and wore badges. Amanda had suggested, more than once, that brains were not automatically connected to either item.

Not that there weren't plenty of cops she admired. Atlanta homicide detective Jim Harrison was one, though she doubted he realized it. She'd be wanting to chat with him first thing, as a matter of fact. Donelli, though he'd long since turned in his gun and his badge in Brooklyn, was another. She wondered if talking the cases over with him would be worth the aggravation of listening to another one of his lectures about caution. He'd been blessedly silent the night before, but she doubted that would last. It never did.

She picked up the morning paper and handed it to Oscar. He tossed it back on her desk.

"I saw the story. Good coverage. What makes you think you can do something the *Constitution* can't?"

Amanda delicately raised her eyebrows.

"Okay, so you're better. I don't doubt that, but why now? Why this murder?"

She recalled Lynette Rogers's friendliness, her concern. "Because I was in the park last night. I was talking to that woman just a couple of hours before her murder was reported. She stopped and offered to stick around while I caught my breath. I should have let her. If I had . . ."

Showing no surprise whatsoever—Donelli or Jenny Lee must have gotten to him ahead of her—Oscar waved off the guilt-ridden statement before it could be completed. "If you had, the killer would have murdered her later, if she was already his target. If he wasn't after her specifically, he would have killed someone else. You couldn't have stopped it, Amanda."

The rational words did nothing to assuage her guilt. "Maybe not, but maybe I can stop the next one, if I can help find this nut. I've already checked the other cases. The first one was eighteen months ago, in the fall. The second one was six months after that, just before Easter. The third was in October. Then one in January, another in March, and now April. They're getting closer together, Oscar. I've read some of the profiles of serial killers. It seems to me this one must be getting desperate."

Amanda took heart from his heavy sigh of resignation.

"I'm not going to talk you out of this, am I?" he said. "I told Joe it would be a waste of time."

"I wondered how long it would be before his name crept into the conversation. What time did he call you last night? About eleven-thirty would be my guess. Do you discuss all of my assignments with him?" she grumbled, taking back all the kind thoughts she'd been having about Donelli since their conversation the night before. "Was the Olympics' construction story his idea?"

He scowled at her. "No, I do not discuss your assignments with him. But maybe you should reconsider."

"Why? Do you have some valid reason why it's not a good story or are you just worried about me?"

"Is worrying about you such a crime?" he inquired indignantly.

She grinned at him, sensing that victory was within reach. "Nope, but it's lousy journalism."

He shook his head. "I don't even know why I try to pretend that I'm the boss around here. Do some checking, if it'll make you happy."

"It will make me very happy."

An hour later Amanda was seated in a coffee shop waiting for Jim Harrison. He'd cursed. He'd argued. But in the end the detective had agreed to tell her what he knew about the six homicides.

Amanda could probably have pulled most of it from previous stories and public records, but she wanted to hear his spin. Occasionally, because they'd worked more or less together in the past, he would divulge things to her that had been kept from other members of the media. She guarded that trust zealously. She knew Jim Harrison was not a man to give his trust lightly, and though he was sometimes exasperated by her aggressive style of reporting, she'd never betrayed him.

Looking rumpled and exhausted, he slid into the booth opposite her. "You couldn't just attend press briefings like everyone else?" he grumbled.

"Why should I, when I have the best source in the department? I'll spring for coffee. You look as if you could use it."

"A cup of coffee won't buy you diddly, Amanda."

"French toast, then? Bacon? Eggs? Grits?"

"You're getting closer. For that I might reveal the name of the victim."

"The *Constitution* had that on page one of the local section. Lynette Rogers. What do you know about her so far?"

He reached for his coffee and drank greedily. Then, as if the caffeine has loosened his tongue, he said, "Not much more than what was in the paper. A little background. She's one of four girls."

"Oldest? Youngest?"

"Second oldest. She was born in a little town not far from Plains, Georgia. Her daddy grows peanuts. Does well enough to have sent all four girls to college. Lynette was in the Miss Georgia contest. She came in second runner-up, took her prize money, and invested it. By the time she left college, she already had something of a reputation as an investor. A brokerage here in Atlanta had her on staff before the ink was dry on her diploma. She married her college sweetheart, a guy by the name of Andrew Stone. He was in PR. Not too successful at it. They were divorced last year."

"She took back her maiden name?"

"Never took his, from what I've been able to find out. She had a real independent streak, wanted her own professional identity."

"Have you talked to him?"

"Can't seem to locate him. Her family says the guy left town a couple of months after the divorce became final, about six, maybe eight months ago. They don't know where he went and don't seem to care. Neither does anyone at any of the firms where he used to work."

"Then the divorce wasn't a friendly parting."

"Not if the complaints we have on file are any indication."

Amanda's head snapped up. "Complaints?"

"The guy had a nasty temper. He'd been harassing her. Her boss called the cops the last time because Stone had turned up at the office, threatened her."

Amanda put down her notebook and regarded Jim Harrison intently. "Is Stone your primary suspect?"

"He's certainly on the short list. I might add that it's a very short list. I've only made a few calls so far, but there hasn't been so much as a negative whisper about this woman. Everybody adored her."

"Except her ex-husband."

"Except her ex-husband," he agreed.

"Or maybe the same guy who killed those other five women," Amanda suggested slowly, watching the detective's face.

Unfortunately, Jim Harrison was too experienced at fending off speculation to show any reaction at all. He didn't even blink.

"Well?" she prodded.

"Amanda, I know patience has never been one of your virtues, but it has been less than twelve hours since her body was discovered. Since no one was found standing over her with a smoking gun, I'm not ruling out anything. I don't even have an exact time of death yet."

"I might be able to help you out there," Amanda said.

He set down his coffee cup very carefully, then leveled a gaze at her. "Meaning?"

"I saw her at about six forty-five, just at dusk. I was running and had a cramp. She stopped to see if I was okay. We talked a couple of minutes, then she went on."

Instantly more alert, he pulled a sketch from his pocket and spread it on the table. "Where in the park?"

Amanda studied the entrances and paths and, after a couple of false starts, located precisely where she'd been when she'd encountered Lynette Rogers. "Here," she said, pointing to the spot with her pen. "Where was the body found?"

Harrison tapped his finger on a curve in the path not two hundred yards away. Amanda shuddered and felt guiltier than ever for not having let Lynette Rogers linger with her.

"Guess that gives us our time of death, then, doesn't it?" he said. "Maybe six forty-eight, six-fifty. Can't get much more precise than that." He drew a notebook from his pocket. "So, Amanda, who else did you see in the park last night?"

She struggled to recall any one person, then finally shrugged. "It was a pleasant night. The park was crowded.

I must have spoken to a dozen or more people and jogged past even more than that. I don't know any of them."

"Any of them men alone? Suspicious-looking? Someone who looked out of place? Uneasy?"

"When I'm out there, the only thing on my mind is breathing. I'm not looking in the shadows."

Clearly disappointed, he snapped the notebook shut and slid it back into his pocket. "Maybe that's something you ought to think about doing," he advised. "If this was just some random attack, you could have been found dead in the bushes just as easily as Lynette Rogers."

For the first time since she'd decided to pursue the story of what was most likely a serial killer, Amanda drew in a deep breath and prayed like crazy that Andrew Stone had been in that park last night. If he'd killed his ex-wife, then she wouldn't have to deal with the survivor's guilt that Jim Harrison had just heaped upon her so unwittingly.

"For the sake of argument, let's say it was the same person who killed those other women. . . . "

"I'm not saying those others were linked, either," he protested, albeit without much conviction.

"I'm saying it, hypothetically."

"Based on what?"

"Gut instinct. Logic. Come on, Detective, you know it has to be more than coincidence when five women about the same age are killed. Six women now. Surely there were similarities about the scene, the killer's MO, something that would trigger an alarm."

He shook his head. "You want to talk gut instinct, I'll go along with you. You want to talk evidence, that's something else. Every one of those women was found in a completely different location. Every one of them was apparently killed by someone who knew their habits. Different times of day. I've gone over their files a thousand times and I can't find one single thing they had in common beyond the superficial fact that all were fairly secure financially and were bright."

"How about robbery as a motive?"

"Nope. Some of them were still wearing expensive jewelry. The ones carrying purses still had money and credit cards intact."

Amanda couldn't recall much about the physical appearances of the women. "Were they all blond like Lynette?"

"Nope."

"Tall?"

"Nope. You're grasping at straws."

"Okay, I haven't been through all the reports yet. Were all of them killed the same way? Mutilated? Raped?"

He hesitated. "No mutilation. No rapes. All of them were strangled or suffocated. Only the Rogers woman had a mark on her. She was the most athletic of them. She probably struggled. She had some cuts. They weren't deep. I'm guessing some sort of switchblade, maybe even one of those fancy pocket knives with all the doodads built in."

"Did you bring along pictures?"

He reached in his bulging pocket and pulled out several folded-up sheets of paper—the missing persons flyers that had been distributed on each of the first five before the discovery of their bodies. Amanda smoothed them out on the table.

Lauren Blakely: A twenty-seven-year-old architect, new to the Atlanta area and member of a prestigious firm, Blakely was the only one of the victims who was married. Large tortoiseshell-rimmed glasses framed eyes the warm color of brandy. Her straight auburn hair was cut chin length and was parted down the center with wispy bangs. There was something a little French about the style.

"She was the first, right?" Amanda asked Harrison, who was polishing off a huge portion of scrambled eggs.

"As far as we know. Her body was found in a wooded area about eighteen months ago. She'd been reported missing about a month earlier by her husband, William Hennessy, also an architect."

"What was your take on Hennessy?"

"He seemed sincerely distraught. Admitted there were problems in the marriage, but he swore they were trying to work them out."

"Did he have an alibi?"

"Since we couldn't pinpoint the time of death exactly, it would be hard to dismiss anything he told us. We can't even say with absolute certainty that she disappeared on the exact day he reported her missing. Maybe he offed her, then waited a couple of days before coming in to tell us she'd vanished," he said with a shrug that dismissed the speculation even as he voiced it.

"You don't believe that, do you?"

"A good cop doesn't believe anything except hard facts. William Hennessy may not have been a perfect husband, for all I know he might even have wanted his wife dead, but I sure couldn't prove he had anything to do with it."

"Is he still under suspicion?"

"Until I close a case everyone who ever came within a fifty-mile radius of the victim is under suspicion. Yeah, I'd say Hennessy is still a strong contender."

"He's still in Atlanta?"

"Oh, yeah. Remarried, in fact."

"Oh, really?" Amanda made a note to track down the architect and see for herself whether his grief had simply run its course or if it had been feigned in the first place. She picked up the next flyer.

Joyce Landers: A twenty-eight-year-old psychotherapist, single, adored by her patients. Serious eyes gazed back from the black-and-white photo, a publicity shot apparently done for the radio call-in show she'd hosted once a week.

Amanda looked up from the photo. "What's the story on her?"

"She was reported missing by several of her patients when she failed to keep their appointments one morning in late March last year. Two weeks later we found her body stashed in the trunk of her car. The car had been abandoned in a parking garage about a block from her office building. It wasn't the garage she normally would have used. The car had been wiped clean of prints."

"Any suspects?"

"We heard rumors that she was involved in a lesbian relationship, but we couldn't find the supposed partner. For a while we focused on one of her patients who had a history of violent behavior, a guy named John Cameron. A couple of patients reported hearing Landers and this

Cameron arguing at the end of a session, then seeing him storm out."

"Where's Cameron now?"

"Back in the psych ward. He flipped out when he heard she was dead. We've tried questioning him, but he slips in and out of reality. Again, there's insufficient evidence to link him to her death."

Amanda moved on to the next flyer. Marnie Evans, MD: A twenty-nine-year-old physician in private practice with a group of family medicine doctors. Her picture revealed a woman whose energy radiated toward the camera. Her short dark brown hair was mussed, and whatever makeup she might have had on at the start of the day had worn off. She looked as if the photographer had snapped the shutter just an instant before she took off running to check on another patient, her stethoscope around her neck, her white lab coat rumpled.

Harrison shook his head. "She's the only one we found at home. She was in the kitchen, dinner still on the stove. Looked as if somebody broke in on her, panicked, and killed her on the spot. Her date called us when he arrived and found the front door ajar."

"Was he a suspect?"

"Yes and no. He had opportunity, but only a fool would call the cops within minutes of killing someone and expect to bluff his way through an interrogation. We couldn't find any motive for the guy to have killed her."

"There must have been somebody else."

He nodded. "The suspect we liked best in that one was a guy she'd hired a few weeks before to work on her lawn. He'd been there that day. The neighbors saw him pulling weeds about an hour before she got home from the office. No one actually saw him go into the house, though, and we didn't find his prints on anything inside except a glass. It works as evidence, but there are plenty of legitimate explanations for that glass being there."

Amanda asked for names and jotted them down. Then she extracted the flyer for the fourth victim.

Daria Winters: A thirty-year-old prosecutor, the oldest of the victims and, based on the color snapshot on the flyer, the most photogenic of them all. Wide, intelligent green eyes were her most dominant feature. Amanda imagined that intense stare could intimidate the most belligerent witness. Ash-brown hair had been lightly frosted and styled by an expert to flatter her high cheekbones.

"You ever work with her?" she asked Harrison.

He nodded. "She was a damned good lawyer. She knew what it took to make a case stick. Some of the cops hated her because she wouldn't go into court until she knew with absolute certainty that she could win. In the end, that meticulous attention to detail paid off. Daria's cases weren't thrown out on technicalities. They weren't shrugged off by juries because of flimsy evidence."

"Your chief suspect?"

"We figured she was done by an ex-con named Otis Franklin. She'd put him away and he'd threatened her repeatedly during the trial and after. He got out of jail just ten days before she disappeared. We worked like hell to make a case against him stick. All the cops wanted this one closed and her killer locked away."

"Obviously you couldn't make it stick."

"Hard to do when the guy was with his parole officer at the time the medical examiner estimates she died."

"He was able to pinpoint the time of death that closely?"

"He gave us a range, on a Friday. Otis and this parole officer liked to bowl. They were at an alley for hours on that particular Friday. Then they went to dinner."

"Isn't that unusual, maybe something a con would do to cover up a crime he'd committed, say, an hour earlier?"

"I'll buy that. A jury wouldn't, not without something else to tie this guy directly to the murder."

Amanda was beginning to get depressed. All of the cases thus far had plausible suspects, even if the police hadn't been able to make the cases stick. She looked at the last flyer.

Betsy McDaniels Taylor: A twenty-seven-year-old heiress, whose body had been found less than two weeks ago. Amanda remembered this case most clearly. The police were able to pinpoint the date she had disappeared from the family estate, wearing the wide-brimmed straw hat, cut-off jeans, and T-shirt she liked to wear when gardening. She had been barefooted.

"Are you still checking out her cousin?" Amanda asked. "Doesn't the guy have a heavy drug habit?"

"Karl Taylor. He claims he's cured. He just got out of a treatment program two months ago. The docs there concur, but they're not likely to admit publicly that the rate of recidivism is pretty high with guys like Taylor. We figure he needed some cash. His cousin turned him down, so he murdered her and ditched her body along the highway out toward Madison. He stood to inherit her trust fund, get access to his own, which she oversaw, plus he could sell off the family heirlooms in the meantime. He'd already hocked a family portrait by some guy who did George Washington."

"Stuart?"

"Yeah, that's the one."

"But you don't have enough for an arrest in this case, either?"

"Not yet," he said wearily. "And now we've got Lynette Rogers."

"If you were me, where would you start?"

He regarded her intently, his expression serious. "You're young, professional, and female. If I were you, Amanda, I'd stay the hell away from this whole scene. If we are dealing with one killer and not the individual suspects we've got in each case, you seem to fit the profile of the victims. If I were you, I wouldn't do anything to draw myself to this guy's attention."

Amanda couldn't resist a rueful grin. "That's what separates you and our favorite FBI agent, Jeffrey Dunne. He'd probably be delighted to set me up as bait."

Harrison swallowed the last of his coffee and reached for his coat. "Why should he bother, when you do it so well all on your own?" he said dryly, then regarded her intently. "Think about what I said, Amanda. I don't like the way this thing feels. I haven't from the very first. You're a damned good reporter, but you're also mortal. Sometimes I think you forget that."

That stark warning delivered, he left her alone with her cold eggs and her suddenly wavering resolve.

C H A P T E R
Three

*I*MPATIENTLY shrugging off her out-of-character uneasiness, Amanda went to the pay phone in the back of the diner and called Jenny Lee at *Inside Atlanta*. Since there was absolutely no possibility of her backing off the story, the best antidote for nervousness was action.

"I need you to track down a guy named Andrew Stone," she told her.

"Isn't he the ex-husband of the woman who was killed last night?"

"That's the one," Amanda said, impressed that Jenny Lee had already begun to memorize pertinent details about the Rogers murder case. "He worked at several PR agencies here in town, but I don't have names. Call them all and see what anyone remembers about him. Maybe somebody can suggest where he might have moved, where he was from originally, things like that. If you run into a dead end, call Donelli. Maybe he can run a skip trace on the guy."

"Donelli, huh?" Jenny Lee said with obvious delight.

She relished any hint that Amanda and Joe might be getting back together. "Unofficially, or should I ask Oscar about paying him?"

"Tell Donelli to send him a bill," she suggested, hoping she'd be around when it arrived. Of course, the price of that amusement would probably be high. Oscar would no doubt hand the invoice straight over to her to pay from her own pocket. Donelli didn't come cheap.

"Amanda honey, you sure do get a charge out of yanking Oscar's chain," Jenny Lee observed. "Where are you going to be while I'm doing your dirty work around here?"

"I thought I'd pay a call on William Hennessy. His wife was the first victim, Lauren Blakely. I checked the Yellow Pages right before I called you. His office is on the north side of town."

She heard Oscar's voice rumbling on the other end of the line, despite Jenny Lee's attempts to muffle the sound.

"What does he want?" Amanda asked, envisioning Oscar trying to snatch the phone away from her researcher.

"*He* wants to know if you're carrying your damned beeper," Oscar snapped in her ear.

"In my purse," she said dutifully.

"Are the batteries in?"

"Yes, Oscar."

"Then why the hell haven't you been returning my calls?"

Amanda dug through her purse and found the silent beeper buried on the bottom, amid some very old, slightly squished jelly beans. It was just possible that the batteries hadn't been changed in all the months the beeper had spent sitting in her desk drawer. "I'll get it checked," she promised. "Why'd you need me?"

"Your pal at the FBI called. He said he woke up with this odd sensation at the back of his neck that you were about to tiptoe onto his turf again. Of course, he also admitted he woke up like that most days."

"So exactly what did Jeffrey Dunne want? Workmen's comp because I'm giving him stress?"

"He would like very much for you to stop by FBI headquarters. He will settle for a phone call. I have the number right here."

"Never mind. It's etched in my brain. If he calls in again, tell him I'll get back to him."

"I think he had in mind sooner rather than later."

"We don't always get what we want in life, do we? Anything else?"

"I also hear Armand LeConte would like to know if you're free to fly to Paris for the weekend," Oscar reported with a definite touch of annoyance. "Would you mind telling me what the hell an international arms merchant is doing inviting you to France?"

Amanda had a pretty good idea about Armand's intentions. He'd expressed them often enough since they'd met several months before during her research into an illegal arms deal. She doubted her decidedly old-fashioned boss was up to hearing them. "He doesn't think anyone in the States can bake a decent croissant. He's been trying to prove it to me."

"Why would you care about a thing like that?"

"I don't. That makes me a challenge. Don't panic, Oscar. I'm not going to defect to *Le Monde* or *Elle*."

"Good thing," he said with an indignant huff. "I've heard you speak French. You couldn't order soup without winding up with calves brains."

A stomach-churning thought. Amanda agreed, though, the less said about her French the better. "Let me talk to Jenny Lee again." She heard the receiver change hands and counted herself lucky that Oscar hadn't wasted precious time lecturing her about Donelli's attributes, just in case she'd forgotten them in a fog of French perfume.

"If a man as sexy as Armand LeConte asked me to fly to Paris, I'd have to think twice about it," Jenny Lee told her. It was an amazing admission given her loyalty to Donelli.

"He asks at least once a week. I can always change my mind," Amanda said breezily, knowing perfectly well that she wouldn't. Armand was dangerous. He was intriguing. But, alas, he wasn't Joe.

"After you've done what you can on Stone, start pulling every single article on the murders you can find," she told Jenny Lee. "See if you can create a chart with everything from time of death to where the body was found, background, et cetera. Do every category you can think of first, then we'll fill in what we know about each woman. Maybe we'll hit some obscure similarities the police missed."

"You mean like they were all Pisces or they all took the same cooking class?"

"Exactly. Let your imagination run wild about anything

young professional women might do, places they might go, groups they might join. Okay?"

"You've got it."

"How about pizza at my place tonight?"

"After we run," Jenny Lee reminded her.

The very thought sent a chill down Amanda's spine. "Jenny Lee, you couldn't get me in that park tonight if you chased me with a rifle."

"We'll see," she replied—a little too smugly, it seemed to Amanda.

William Hennessy, unlike his reportedly successful late wife, apparently did not have the wherewithal for a lavish life-style. In fact, if his one-man architectural firm was anything to judge by, he didn't even bother with keeping up appearances.

Amanda found the address in a strip mall that had lost half its tenants when a major shopping center had sprawled across several acres down the road. The front window hadn't been washed since the last rains had splattered it with mud. He hadn't bothered naming the business. A hand-lettered sign on the glass door proclaimed in a simple, straightforward way, *William Hennessy, Architect*.

Though she couldn't see any signs of life inside, other than a light on over a drawing board, Amanda tried the door. It opened, admitting her to an eerily hushed room, littered with blueprints and throw-away coffee cups. The linoleum on the floor had long since lost any hint of shine to streaks of scuff marks and muddy splotches.

"Be right with you," a deep, masculine voice called from the back.

Amanda used the time to study the sketch on the drawing board. It was for an addition to a house. It was nothing fancy, just four walls, simple sash windows—the kind of addition that might be made on a shoestring to accommodate an expanding family. She wondered if William Hennessy had always lacked imagination and had lived in the shadow of his more talented wife, or if he'd simply faded into the background after the murder to avoid drawing attention to himself.

The man who eventually emerged from the back surprised her. He was dressed in perfectly pressed slacks from an obviously expensive suit. There wasn't a wrinkle in his white shirt, except where the sleeves had been rolled up. His tie was knotted as precisely as some lawyer's in a downtown high-rise. His brown hair, streaked gold by the sun, was a touch too long but otherwise neatly combed. Unusual blue eyes ringed with brown gazed at her, in confusion.

"Obviously you're not Greg Cahill," he said, striding across the office to hold out his hand. An appealingly boyish smile broke across his face. "Hi, I'm William Hennessy."

"Amanda Roberts."

He studied her an instant. "I recognize that name. Have we met?"

She shook her head. "I'm a reporter. I write for *Inside Atlanta*."

If her identity made him nervous, he hid it well. In fact,

he looked downright intrigued. "Yeah, that's right. I've read your stuff. Enjoyed it."

"Thanks."

"So what brings you here? You building a new house?"

"Afraid not. I'm working a story."

A little of the color drained out of his face. "The murders," he said in a voice that had turned as flat as day-old champagne. "When I saw the paper this morning, I knew it was going to start all over again."

She nodded. "I'm sorry to bring up painful memories, but it's important. Can you spare a few minutes?"

He looked as if he'd like to say no, but he didn't. He gestured toward a chair. "We can talk until Cahill gets here. I can't afford to turn away prospective clients these days."

"Times are tough?"

"No tougher for me than anyone else. People don't do the kind of building I like to do when the economy's sour."

"What kind is that?"

"Custom, environmentally sensitive houses. If you do it right, you don't have to do it over every five or ten years. People would rather save a little up front, skimp on materials."

It sounded like the beginning of a frequent discourse. Amanda wasn't especially interested in learning more about people's shortsightedness. She already had a pretty good fix on it anyway. She'd spent the last month trying to get a poorly installed electrical system repaired without ripping half her house apart. The electrician's tongue had clicked disapprovingly as he'd worked. She figured each click added another hundred dollars to the bill. Her only consolation had been the fact that her landlord was obligated to pay it.

William Hennessy sighed. "You didn't come here to hear about that, though, did you? You want to talk about Lauren."

"Right. What was she like?"

"She was one of the best and brightest in our class," he said without hesitation. "She was the one who was courted by all the big firms. She picked Atlanta because she thought it had all sorts of possibilities as a city of tomorrow. She liked doing both splashy high rises and renovations. Most architects prefer one or the other, but Lauren wasn't typical. She didn't conform. Hell, she chose me and I wasn't exactly destined for the same fast track she was on."

"Were you competitive?"

He shook his head. "Never. We had different interests, architecturally speaking. I was proud of her. She understood my goals, as well. I think she respected them."

"Even so, your marriage was in trouble." She made it a statement, not a question. He didn't even try to deny it.

"We hit a rocky patch. I was ready for kids. She wasn't. We went to counseling to try to resolve the differences. Before we could, she died. I believe that we would have made it, though."

Amanda listened for a discordant note, some tiny hint that William Hennessy was simply putting the best face on things for her benefit. She didn't hear it. He sounded absolutely sincere.

"You're remarried now?"

He grinned. "Done your homework, I see. Yes. And before you ask, I didn't know Risa before. We met about thirteen months ago. Got married two months later."

"And she shares your desire to have a family?"

"She's pregnant."

"Congratulations," she said automatically, then paused to listen for the sound of her own biological clock ticking. It was blessedly silent. At least that was one kind of angst she was being spared now that she'd passed her thirtieth birthday. Every time she saw Donelli lately, though, she wondered how long that would last. She kept seeing little brown-eyed, dark-haired miniatures, their skin tanned from playing outdoors, their smiles every bit as devastating as their daddy's, their voices accented with hints of Brooklyn and a soft southern drawl. She saw those kids, saw Donelli with them, but she couldn't for the life of her put herself into the picture.

She forced her attention back to the man seated comfortably across from her. His posture was relaxed, his whole attitude unintimidated. If he was shaken by her unannounced arrival on his doorstep or by her questions about Lauren Blakely's murder, he was covering it every bit as smoothly as any con artist she'd ever met . . . including her own ex-husband, Mack Roberts. Just thinking of Mack reminded her that people were not always what they seemed to be. She injected a necessary note of caution into her appraisal of William Hennessy.

"You reported your wife missing, didn't you?" she asked.

He nodded.

"How long after you discovered that she'd disappeared?"

Judging from his defensive expression, he didn't mistake her meaning.

"I called the police not five minutes after I woke up and realized she hadn't come home all night."

"Her staying out was that unusual? I know people who have late night meetings, then wind up sleeping in their offices on occasion."

"Overnight? Never," he said adamantly. "Lauren was a workaholic, but we had an agreement that no matter what, we would both be back at the house by ten o'clock. We wanted to have at least an hour or two together to unwind. She rarely broke that commitment by more than a few minutes, maybe an hour."

"Why didn't you call the police at ten oh-five, then? Or eleven o'clock?"

"I got home about nine that night. Lauren had left a message that she was caught up in a meeting that was running late, but would be home by ten-thirty or eleven. I took a shower, climbed into bed, and turned on the TV to wait. I guess I fell asleep. It was six A.M. when I woke up, with the TV still on, and realized she still wasn't there."

"Who was the meeting with?"

He closed his eyes and shook his head. "I have no idea. It wasn't on her calendar. No one at work knew, either."

"Could it have been something other than business?"

"If you mean dinner with friends, I don't think so. No one ever came forward, anyway. If you mean an affair, the answer is no. Lauren came from a very religious background. She took our wedding vows very seriously. She might eventually have agreed to a divorce, but she would never have cheated on me as long as we were still married."

Amanda focused on one part of his reply, the kind of slip that might have suggested a motive for murder. "Had you asked for a divorce?"

He looked startled by the question. "No. Why?"

"You said she might have given you one *eventually*."

"I just meant that if we hadn't been able to resolve things, she might have reconciled herself to the idea that divorce was our only option. She wouldn't have come to that decision easily, though."

Again Amanda listened for the discordant note, the hint of quick-on-his-feet dissembling. It wasn't there. William Hennessy, if anything, sounded disconcertingly honest, anxious to clarify and cooperate.

He did glance at his watch, though, and Amanda recalled the client he'd been expecting, probably at least a half hour ago. When he saw the time, a little of the energy seemed to seep out of him. It was as if all too many prospective clients had made appointments and never kept them. She found the thought of all those dashed hopes incredibly depressing.

"I won't hold you up any longer," she said. "I might want to talk to you again, though."

"Sure. Anytime," he said, sounding defeated.

Amanda tried to think of something, anything, she could say to cheer him up. Nothing came to mind. An oppressive silence hung in the air between them as she went to the door. Her hand was on the knob when he finally spoke.

"Look, I know the police probably still consider me a suspect, but I didn't do it," he said, his expression earnest. "I want to see Lauren's killer caught as much as anyone, probably more so since there's a cloud of suspicion hanging over my head. If you can do that, I'll be grateful. I still think about where they found her, out on that road, all alone. I have nightmares about how frightened she must have been before she died."

"Is there one single person in Lauren's life who might have had a motive to kill her? Anyone whose toes she'd stepped on professionally? Anyone she'd rejected to marry you? Anyone who stood to gain from her death?"

There was a wry twist to his lips as he shook his head. "I wish I could manufacture another strong suspect for you, but everyone loved Lauren, Ms. Roberts." He paused and looked directly into her eyes. "Including me."

C H A P T E R

Four

*T*HEY looked like a damned parade, Amanda thought in disgust as she jogged along behind Jenny Lee a couple of hours after her relatively unproductive interview with William Hennessy. A hundred feet or so in front of Jenny Lee and careful not to get too far ahead were Donelli and *Inside Atlanta*'s favorite free-lance photographer, Larry Carter. Amanda was certain only his fear of a heart attack had kept Oscar from bringing up the rear.

"You're very sneaky, Jenny Lee," Amanda grumbled.

"Thank you."

"It wasn't a compliment."

That familiar smug smile flitted across the twenty-four-year-old's face. "You're running, aren't you? And you're getting a chance to peek at the scene of the crime again."

"Okay, yes," she said grudgingly. "But bodyguards?"

"Well, now, that just sort of happened," Jenny Lee claimed, her expression all innocence. "I mentioned to

Larry that we were going for a run then having pizza. You
know how he feels about pizza."

"I know how he feels about being left out of anything
involving you these days."

Jenny Lee smiled demurely. "True. Anyway, he just
happened to talk to Donelli."

"Who exploded," Amanda guessed based on the scowl
he'd had on his face ever since he'd stomped into the
house a half hour earlier wearing sweats and sneakers.

"He said it was the worst damned fool idea any of us
had ever had, but since he was sure there was no stopping
us, he'd come along."

"A wise man, Mr. Donelli."

"Cute, too," Jenny Lee observed, gazing pointedly at
the man in question. "Just look at those buns."

"Jenny Lee!"

"He's not as cute as Larry, though," she said loyally.

"I heard that," the photographer called over his shoulder.

Amanda had no doubt that Donelli had heard every
word as well. She wondered if he was flattered by Jenny
Lee's assessment of his ass or too exasperated with the lot
of them to care how sexy any of them found him. Including her. Mostly her.

He turned just then, though, and winked at her. "Enjoy-
ing the view?"

"Jenny Lee's just giving you guys a taste of your own
medicine," Amanda said as he dropped back and fell into
step beside her. "You've been doing that sort of thing to
women for years."

"Me personally? I wasn't aware you knew my habits

prior to the past couple of years. Since we met, I can almost guarantee I have not publicly commented on any other woman's buns."

Amanda glowered at him. "But I know how you think."

"Lasciviously?"

"Bingo."

"That's what happens when you've been banished to a cold, lonely bed for months."

Amanda ignored that remark because she wasn't entirely ready to deal with any changes in their physical relationship just yet. They were still mending the mistakes that had left their emotional rapport in tatters. First things first.

Fortunately they were nearing the place along the path where she had met Lynette Rogers the previous night. Something in her expression must have communicated her discomfort to Donelli.

"This the place?" he asked.

Amanda nodded and gestured to a grassy spot on the right up ahead. "I was over there, trying to catch my breath, when she stopped and asked if I needed any help."

Donelli dropped his teasing and immediately slowed his pace. "How long had you been off the path when she came along?"

"A minute or two. The stitch in my side hadn't gone away and I was still huffing and puffing."

"I think we can rule out a random attack, then."

"Why?"

"You'd have made a much easier target. You wouldn't have been able to put up much of a fight just then."

"True," she admitted. A chill ran through her just think-ing about it.

"Let's say the guy was focused on Lynette, then. Was she well into her run or just starting?"

"She looked as if she'd just started, but she was a marathoner. She could probably go for an hour without mussing her hair. Why?"

"I just wondered if he had targeted her outside the park, then followed her in off the street, or if he already knew her route and was waiting to catch her when she was tired out."

Amanda hadn't thought about that. One implied an ac-cidental encounter, albeit one that had taken place some-where other than the site of the murder. The other indicated premeditation. Had Lynette said anything that might give her a clue if she was about to end the run? If so, she couldn't recall it. "I don't have any idea," she said finally, then recalled that her hair, though neat enough in that ponytail, had looked damp. She described it to Donelli.

"Good. Now where was the body found?"

"Just around the bend, back in the bushes, if I under-stood Jim Harrison's map."

"Was it crowded in this part of the park?"

Amanda shook her head. "Not by then. It was almost dusk."

"So, more than likely it was the end of her run. Even a dedicated runner, if she's as smart as this woman report-edly was, wouldn't be taking chances in this part of the park after dark. There's still a lot of activity on the tennis courts and ball fields then, but not around here."

Amanda nodded slowly. "I see your point. That makes the likelihood that the killer knew her greater."

"Greater, but not surefire certain. Hell, he could have been a stalker, who'd just watched her from afar."

"I wish you wouldn't do that."

"What?"

"Set up a scenario and then shoot it down."

He grinned. "You do that all the time. How many suspects have you put on a list, then turned right around and dismissed?"

"Because careful analysis proves they aren't solid suspects."

"No, because you dismissed their guilt from some gut instinct. Now tell me about William Hennessy."

"You mean the fact that he's not guilty," she said dryly.

He lifted his gaze heavenward. "See what I mean? Fill me in on the facts and let me make up my own mind."

Before Amanda could do that, a kid on Rollerblades swept past them, almost knocking Jenny Lee down as she scrambled to get out of his way. A burly man, who looked to be in his late thirties or early forties, his face dangerously flushed, tore after him, clearly without much hope of catching up. Just when it seemed that the kid's escape was certain, his skates hit a crack in the pavement and sent him sprawling.

The man latched on to the kid's arm and hauled him to his feet. As his eyes filled with panic, the boy aimed one Rollerblade-clad foot straight at the man's shin. It failed to connect only because the man's reflexes were surprisingly quick.

"I'm not going back and that's that," the boy shouted,

trying to jerk his skinny arm free from the man's beefy grasp. "I'm not."

Donelli strolled over to the struggling pair. He nodded politely at the man. To Amanda's astonishment, he addressed him by name.

"Hey, Bryce. What's the problem?"

The man, who was still struggling to catch his breath, eventually managed to say, "Kid's run away from home."

"His family hire you to look for him?"

"My family doesn't give a shit about me," the boy said, his shoulders sagging in defeat.

Amanda wondered about that. His Rollerblades were expensive. His jeans looked new, and his jacket appeared to be real leather. Middle-class kids could be neglected, but this boy looked well clothed and well fed. She had a hunch his thin frame was due more to a sudden spurt of adolescent growth than any lack of food.

As she watched, his expression turned calculating, a look normally associated with adults trying to cut a deal. His gaze went from Joe to this Bryce and back again. He apparently opted for trusting Donelli. He shot him an appealing glance. "Can you get this jerk off me?"

Donelli shrugged. "Depends."

"On?"

"You telling me the truth. Why'd you leave home?"

"I told you. Nobody there gave a damn about me."

"When did you leave?"

"Last night."

"You've been gone over night?"

"So what? I ain't scared."

"I'm sure you're not. You are a little young to be on your own, though."

"I'm old enough."

"Ten?"

"Shit, no. I'm twelve."

Donelli nodded. "Definitely old enough not to want people to worry about you. If you're gonna be a grown-up, you have to take responsibility for your actions."

The boy sighed in exasperation. "I told you—"

"That nobody cares. If that's true, why'd they hire somebody to look for you?"

"Because it wouldn't look good if it got out that a politician's son skipped out on his lousy parents."

He said it with such weary cynicism that Amanda felt unexpected tears spring into her eyes. She walked over. "What's your name?"

He eyed her warily. "Pete. What's yours?"

"Amanda," she said. "You know, Pete, we were about to go to my house for some pizza. Why don't you come along and we can all talk about this? Maybe you'll decide that calling home and letting your parents know you're okay would be the right thing to do."

Bryce glared at her. "I've got an obligation to get this kid back home."

"Then don't blow your best shot at it," Donelli said quietly. He looked down at Pete. "How about it? Pizza sound good?"

"Yeah, I guess."

His agreement added two more to the parade that was now straggling back toward Amanda's house. Donelli introduced the man as Bryce Cummings, a former cop and now an Atlanta PI.

"His father is Pete Jackson, right?" Donelli asked. "Kid looks just like him. Has the same kind of mouth, too. All tough talk."

Bryce laughed. "Yeah. I thought so, too. We ran into each other a few times when I was on the force. I worked private security for him at a couple of campaign parties. When the kid skipped out last night, the father called me."

Donelli's gaze went to the boy, who was quizzing Larry on his ever-present camera. "Any truth to what the boy said?"

Bryce held up his hands. "Hey, I don't make judgments. My job was to find the kid. I did that. When I turn him over to his parents, I collect my check. That's it. No involvement."

"What about the mother?" Amanda asked, wishing she'd spent more time studying local politics in Atlanta. All she remembered about Jackson was that he was serving his second term at City Hall and that there hadn't been any scandals in his political career so far. "Do you know her?"

A faint smile tugged at the private investigator's lips. "Now, she's something. Talks like an old-fashioned southern belle. Calls everyone '*sugar*' and has a drink in your hand before you've got your coat off. Wears all these soft clothes that kinda float. Reminds me of a ghost drifting by. I've heard, though, that she's tough as nails."

"Is Pete an only child?"

"Nope. Oldest of three. His old man says he's been

trouble ever since he learned to talk. You heard him. The kid does have a mouth on him."

"Talking tough is not the same as being bad," Donelli said. "It usually hides a whole lot of hurt."

Something in Joe's voice caught Amanda's attention. Had he known other kids like Pete? Or had his own childhood been troubled in some way he'd never revealed?

"Say, Amanda," Pete said, skating over to her side. "This pizza, is it going to have pepperoni on it?"

"It's going to have everything on it."

He regarded her with a look that was entirely too adult. "You and me, I think we could have something going here."

"Oh, really?" she said, careful to keep her amusement out of her voice. "And what would that be?"

"You seeing anybody?"

"As a matter of fact, I am."

He cast a look at Donelli. "Him?"

"Him," Amanda agreed.

"Figures."

"Why is that?"

"The dude's cool. Even I can see that."

Amanda glanced up at Donelli just in time to catch his attention. A slow smile spread across his face, warming her. She turned back to Pete. "Definitely a cool dude," she agreed.

An hour and a half later, when they were all stuffed with pizza, Donelli looked at Pete. "So, what do you think? You want to give your folks a call? Or maybe have Bryce here give you a lift home?"

"It's up to me?" Pete asked, his wariness evident.

"You say you're old enough to make your own decisions. I respect that."

Pete struggled with the concept of trust. It was fairly obvious that it was new to him. "Okay, here's the deal," he said finally.

Donelli fought to contain a grin. "Yes?"

"I'll let the man here take me home, if you and me can maybe stay in touch. Get together once in a while." He glanced at Amanda. "You too."

Amanda exchanged a look with Donelli. "I think we can work that out, don't you?"

"No problem," Joe agreed. He pulled a business card from his pocket and handed it to Pete. "You call anytime."

The boy shot a look of disdain at Bryce. "Let's get it over with, man."

The private eye shook his head. "I gotta stop taking cases like this."

When the two were gone, it was several minutes before anyone spoke. Then Jenny Lee said, "That kid breaks my heart. He sounds like he's all alone in the world."

"But he's not," Larry reminded her.

"I wonder what goes on at that house of his, though," Amanda said. She glanced at Joe. "I don't suppose you'd want to check around a little, see what his family's like?"

He reached over and squeezed her hand. "I was already planning on it. Now in the meantime, why don't we see what we know about these murders?"

"Let's go out on the deck. I'm feeling claustrophobic in here," Amanda said.

"It's freezing out there," Jenny Lee protested.

"Pull on your sweatshirt," Amanda said. "I'll make coffee."

"I'll keep you warm," Larry offered.

Jenny Lee's expression brightened. She even helped make the coffee. Then she and Amanda joined Donelli and Larry on the deck, which had been the house's primary selling point. It overlooked a yard filled with dogwoods in bloom.

"So, talk to me," Donelli said. "What do you have so far?"

What they knew was precious little, though Jenny Lee had started her chart and had calls out all over town looking for some sign of Andrew Stone.

"Last anyone had heard, Stone was heading for Ohio," she said. "I checked information in Cleveland, Columbus, Cincinnati, and Dayton. Nothing. I'll check Akron, Toledo, and the other major cities tomorrow. I figure if he did go to Ohio, he won't be in some little town. He'll need a place big enough to support public relations companies."

"Unless he's decided to change careers or is living in a suburb," Amanda said. "Joe?"

It was all she needed to say. He nodded.

"I'll do a check with the Department of Motor Vehicles tomorrow and see what I come up with."

Amanda picked up the huge poster board that Jenny Lee had used to create her chart. "Anything here?"

Jenny Lee shook her head. "Nothing. They lived in different parts of town, travelled in different circles. One belonged to a health club. One was a marathoner and trained in her spare time. Two of them played tennis, but at different courts. They didn't belong to the same professional associations or any other groups I could find. Probably didn't have time. I even asked some of their friends about favorite restaurants. Only one came up more than once."

It wasn't much, but Amanda was ready to grasp at straws. "Which one?"

"McDonald's."

Amanda groaned. "Terrific."

"That's okay," Donelli said. "None of that is wasted effort. It eliminates what could be a lot of false starts. I'd suggest you concentrate on the two most recent cases, Lynette Rogers and who was the other one?"

"Betsy McDaniels Taylor."

"Right. Focus on them. The trails aren't cold yet. Treat them independently for a day or two. See what you come up with. I'll try to track down the ex-husband tomorrow."

"Can you check the airlines to see if he came or left in the days right before or after Lynette was murdered?" Larry suggested. "Maybe tomorrow night I can go for a run in the park again and see who's around, maybe ask some questions about the regular joggers."

"Good idea," Amanda concurred. "I'll take a drive down to talk to Lynette's family. Jenny Lee, you take a look at the Taylor will to see who stood to gain from her death. Then see what you can find out about that cousin of hers, Karl Taylor. Find out where he went for his drug treatment. See if he—"

A distinct, nearby whisper of sound froze the rest of the suggestion in Amanda's throat. In less than a heartbeat, she envisioned the killer creeping closer, listening to their speculation, mowing them all down with an automatic weapon. Instead what she heard was an all-too-familiar voice.

"Well, well, well, I see the gang's all here."

The dry comment came from the shadows. No one did sarcasm quite as well as Jeffrey Dunne.

"I see I'm too late for damage control," he observed, settling onto an empty chair. "You're already in this up to your eyeballs, aren't you, Amanda?"

"Still sneaking around, aren't you, Agent Dunne?" she said irritably.

"That's '*Special Agent*' Dunne to you," he retorted. "Or Jeffrey." He lifted a hand in Donelli's direction. "Hey, Joe."

"Jeff."

"Is that coffee you all are drinking?"

"I'll get you one," Jenny Lee offered.

It was a wise move on her part. Amanda probably would have dumped it over his head.

"You involved in this case?" Donelli asked the FBI agent.

"Now if I admitted that, I would be admitting that we think we're dealing with a serial killer, wouldn't I?"

"That would certainly be one interpretation," Donelli agreed.

"Let me put it this way. I am not involved personally with these cases."

"Ah, a messenger yet again," Amanda observed. "That must really irk you, *Special* Agent Dunne."

He leaned forward. There was no mistaking the flash of anger in his usually serene expression.

"No, what really irks me, Amanda, is your infantile refusal to admit that some things are more important than the media's right to access every piece of information in the universe on demand. I thought perhaps you'd learned the meaning of the word *ethics* when you actually held off on that last story rather than endangering lives. Now I'm wondering if that wasn't some sort of fluke."

Amanda heard Jenny Lee's gasp, Joe's indrawn breath, and then the collective silence as everyone awaited her reaction to the unwarranted attack. In her own damned backyard, yet! She was on her feet, towering over him, a feat she could accomplish only because he was seated.

"For a man who arrived uninvited, a man who is taking advantage of my hospitality, a man who very nearly cost me the man that I love, you have one helluva lot of nerve talking to me about ethics," she said, her voice climbing.

"Amanda," Joe said softly.

She ignored the warning and continued to glare down at the agent. He looked amazingly unaffected by her tirade. Since he clearly hadn't gotten the message, she snapped, "Why don't you just say whatever you've got to say and get out."

He chuckled. "After you've made me feel so welcome?"

Amanda sighed and sat back down. There were fleeting instants when she actually liked Jeffrey Dunne. This didn't happen to be one of them. "You are very irritating. You know that, don't you?"

"If I don't, I'm sure you'll be more than happy to remind me."

"I consider it my duty."

"Friends?" he inquired.

"Don't press it, Dunne. Why are you here? How'd you even know I was working on these murders?"

"Lucky guess," he said, then drew something out of his pocket. "And this confirmed it."

Amanda reached for it, but Joe snatched it out of Dunne's hand.

"What is it?" she demanded.

"A warning. It turned up at headquarters not twenty minutes ago. Thought I'd bring it straight over."

Amanda could tell from Joe's ashen complexion that she wasn't going to like the contents. "Okay, spill it. What's it say?"

Joe and Special Agent Dunne exchanged a look. Jenny Lee turned a worried gaze toward Larry. It was the FBI agent who finally spoke.

"The note suggests that a certain snooping reporter is in grave danger of becoming victim number seven."

CHAPTER

Five

"*O*BVIOUSLY the killer doesn't know you nearly as well as we do," Jeffrey Dunne commented as the rest of them sat there in stunned silence. "He seems to think the warning will scare you off."

"You say 'the' killer as if it's a given that there's only one," Amanda said, pouncing on the slip.

"'A' killer, then," he corrected quickly.

In Amanda's view an admission was an admission, no matter how fast he tried to take it back. Judging from the resigned expression on his face, he knew that, too.

"Since we all know that you don't scare easily, we could make use of the fact that you've caught his attention," Dunne said eventually.

"You want to use me?" she said incredulously, though why she was surprised was beyond her, given her past history with the FBI.

"No way," Donelli said. "Absolutely not."

Amanda thought it was an awfully adamant objection,

given his own role in making use of her the last time the
FBI had wanted someone to do their dirty work.

"At least this time, I'm asking," Dunne reminded them.
"Let's face it, Amanda, if you're going to report this story,
the killer apparently won't be happy whether you link up
with us or not. You'll still be in danger. We'll still be
watching. It would be helpful if we could work together."

The very idea went against everything Amanda believed in. "You want to watch, watch. I can't stop you, but
I will not join forces with you. It's unethical, for one
thing."

"Is it? What's more important? Catching a man who's
killed six times, maybe more, or preserving that well-de-
veloped independent streak of yours?"

"This isn't about me, dammit. It's about journalists. We
need to remain impartial and objective. We need to be
outsiders. Is any of this getting through to you? We can't
turn government operative when it suits us—or you—and
expect anyone to believe a word we write," she said indignantly.

He shrugged as if her decision neither surprised nor
bothered him. "I told 'em you wouldn't go for it."

"Then why'd you waste time asking?"

"You know how it is when the man in charge gets a notion in his head. All the logic in the world doesn't matter.
In the end, you do what you're told."

"Maybe *you* do," she shot back.

"Amanda, I didn't come here to balance my code of
ethics against yours." He took a final swallow of his coffee, tucked the threatening note into his pocket, and stood
up. " 'Night, folks."

He left the deck, then paused . . . in the shadows again. "Amanda, be careful, you hear?"

She heard the note of genuine concern in his voice, recognized it from other times when he'd lost patience with her but never stopped worrying about the outcome of her impetuous streak. "I always am," she called after him, and heard his wry chuckle.

"I think that's what troubles me the most," he said. "You actually think that you are."

When he'd gone, Amanda looked directly at Jenny Lee and Larry. "We are not going to tell Oscar about this. Understand?" She turned and leveled a gaze at Donelli. "Okay?"

"He has a right to know," Joe countered.

"He does, Amanda," Jenny Lee concurred.

"He'll just worry himself into a frenzy," she contradicted.

"Are you worried about that or are you just afraid he'll pull you off the story?" Joe asked.

"I am worried about his health, dammit. You know he's a heart attack waiting to happen," she retorted. "Besides, he knows there would be no point in pulling me off this assignment. I'd just quit and free-lance it to somebody else."

"Guys, I think we're missing the most important thing here," Larry said finally. "The threat of Amanda's investigation into these murders has finally gotten the killer to make a mistake. He's practically confessed to the FBI that he's responsible for all six of them."

"That's true," Jenny Lee said. "We know for sure now that we're dealing with a serial killer."

Amanda looked at her excited assistant and shook her head. "Why don't I find that the least bit reassuring?"

At the crack of dawn Amanda drove toward Plains. She took the interstate, since everyone agreed it wouldn't be wise to travel alone on Route 19. She'd been adamant about going alone. The others all had angles of their own to pursue that were more important than baby-sitting her.

Even after that disconcerting note, no one had wasted any energy trying to convince her to back off. They had agreed that they should proceed investigating each murder as if it were unique. Then they would see where the lives of the women might have touched, which traits they might have shared that would make them the target of one killer rather than separate murderers.

She drove up to the ranch-style farmhouse between Plains and Americus a couple of hours later, just as half a dozen people emerged and headed toward the two cars parked in the driveway. An older man, his face weathered by the sun, his suit an uncomfortable fit, waited as she walked over.

"Mr. Rogers?"

His head bobbed. "Ma'am."

Amanda told him about the story she was working on. "I'd like to talk to you and your family about Lynette, if that's possible."

Tears shimmered in his weary eyes. "We're on our way to the funeral parlor. This isn't the best time."

"Are services today?"

"No. We have to see the undertaker. Make the arrangements. The police released her body this morning." He swallowed hard, his Adam's apple rising and falling in his throat. "We—" His voice broke. "We haven't seen her. The wife, she needs that. Can't believe our little girl is gone."

"I know it must be very hard," she said, feeling that uneasy sense of being a vulture that came to her occasionally when she was cutting too deeply into a person's private grief. She wished she'd thought before she'd left Atlanta what this day would be like for Lynette's family. She might have postponed the visit. *Might have.* The truth was, she wouldn't have. At the height of stress people tended to reveal the raw truth, if only the reporter was patient enough to wait for it. Most people needed someone to talk to, an objective listener who wouldn't become distraught as they shared their grief.

"I could stay here. We could talk when you get back," she suggested. "If it wouldn't be too much of an imposition."

He glanced toward the car, as if it were a decision he didn't want to be held accountable for making on his own. Just choosing to eat or not eat at a time like this was a chore, though. Amanda had seen the reaction a lot when faced with the survivors of a tragedy.

"I suppose," he said finally, when it was clear there'd be no help from the others.

"Thank you."

"Can't say when we'll be back, exactly. You understand that."

"Of course. You take your time. Would you mind if I waited inside, used your phone? I'll use my phone card for the calls."

He nodded. "Go on in. Door's open."

At her look of amazement, he shrugged. "Ain't much to steal, and folks around here are pretty trusting. Not like Atlanta these days."

"No," she said, not mistaking his meaning. Atlanta, the city that allowed innocent young women to be killed. She reached out and touched his hand, which hung loosely at his side. "I truly am sorry about your daughter."

He didn't even acknowledge her words. He just turned and folded his tall, spare frame into the car. Amanda remained in the driveway as that poor, sad man and his family drove away to make arrangements to bury their daughter.

Though she had permission to go inside, Amanda hesitated on the porch, trying to envision Lynette in this environment. The dogwood trees were blooming in the woods across the road, putting a blaze of pink and white across the horizon. Along the edges of the house azalea bushes echoed the colors of the dogwood. An aging swing, no more than a board and ropes, dangled from a giant oak tree in the side yard. The house itself, of solid brick, was comfortable but hardly fancy.

That was the same impression she'd gotten of Lynette's father—solid, comfortable. With a sigh as she thought of the telltale moisture in his eyes, she opened the screen door and went inside the house.

Oak floors were covered with old-fashioned rag rugs. The concentric circles of tightly wound material appeared handmade, the rainbow of colors faded from repeated washings. The Early American furniture was simple and well worn. A desk, the only piece that looked as if it might be classified an antique, had its own place of honor in the center of the wall at the end of the room.

Inside the desk's glass-fronted cabinet, framed pictures sat on the shelves. School pictures. Snapshots. A formal family portrait. From far too many of them Lynette's intelligent gaze stared back at Amanda. A lump formed in her throat as she thought of all the wasted promise. Finally, when she could bear it no longer, she had to force herself to turn away, realizing as she did that there had been no wedding picture. Whatever mementos there had been of the failed marriage had been packed away.

Guessing that one drawer of the desk probably held yet more photographs, Amanda was sorely tempted to investigate. Instead she went in search of the phone. She found one finally in the kitchen. Using her calling card number, she dialed the office and asked for Jenny Lee.

"How's it going?"

"I hit a dead end on Stone," Jenny Lee announced. "Donelli's working on it from his end. I did find out a little about Karl Taylor. The drug treatment program he was in was out in California. Very expensive. His cousin was footing the bills. Police records show he was picked up for possession of cocaine again about six weeks ago. Apparently the treatment didn't take nearly as well as he'd have everyone believe. You want me to go talk to him?"

"No. I want to see him. I need to get a feel for the house, see where Betsy Taylor was right before she vanished."

"You heading back this way soon?"

"Probably not for a couple of hours. I got here just as

Lynette's family was leaving to make funeral arrangements. I'm waiting for them to get back now."

"How awful."

"It is pretty dismal around here," she confessed. "Look, I'm going to try to catch Donelli. You keep working on that chart. Sooner or later something's bound to click."

Jenny Lee didn't sound convinced, but she promised to persist. A call to Donelli got only his answering machine. Amanda wanted to believe he'd gotten lucky and gone out to pursue a lead. Chances were, though, that he was planting beans. She swallowed an exasperated curse and wandered back into the living room just in time to hear a car drive up.

Relieved that her wait was about over, she walked to the window and glanced out. To her surprise, the car in the driveway wasn't at all familiar. Sleek and black, it looked foreign and expensive.

As she watched, a man finally emerged, looked around the farm much as she had earlier, then approached the front door. With the air of someone familiar with the family's habits, he didn't even hesitate, just opened the door and walked inside. The actions were neither surreptitious nor even cautious. A family member? A neighbor? Whatever, nothing in his demeanor suggested to Amanda that she ought to dive behind the sofa and hide.

"Hello," she said, stepping into view.

Blue eyes as clear as a summer sky met hers. No hint of suspicion there, just friendly interest. "Well, hello, yourself. Who are you?"

"I'm a reporter from Atlanta. Amanda Roberts." She held out her hand. "And you?"

He didn't answer at first. Nor did he seem startled by her identity.

"Down here spying on the bereaved?" he inquired in a pleasant tone that was an odd counterpoint to the derisive nature of the question.

"Actually, they're out. At the funeral home. They said I could wait."

"I see."

Amanda began to wonder if he was a reporter as well. Surely she wasn't the first or the last who'd be visiting Lynette's parents over the next days and weeks. "Are you related to the family?" she prodded.

He shrugged. "I suppose, in a way."

"What way is that?"

"I was married to the recently departed," he said.

Amanda's heart seemed to pound a little harder. She wasn't surprised at all when he added, "I'm Andrew Stone."

But suddenly she wasn't quite so wild about being all alone in the middle of nowhere with this particular stranger.

C H A P T E R

Six

*T*ALK, Amanda's brain told her—with some urgency, in fact. She'd always believed that talking could slow down murderous intent. Not that Andrew Stone seemed particularly threatening. It was the circumstances, the doubts, that made her wish like crazy that he was still safely in Ohio or wherever he'd been for the past few months. Donelli would have found him sooner or later, and she could have questioned him by phone. Long distance.

His silence was really getting on her nerves. He seemed to be aware of it, too, and clearly found it amusing. So she popped a bracing tangerine jelly bean, and then she did what her brain had instructed her to do. She talked.

"You know," she began very casually, "I've been trying to reach you. No one seemed to know where you were."

"Obviously you weren't asking the right people," he said in a smug way that carried an odd edge to it. It was as if he were deliberately taunting her.

Amanda decided she didn't like Andrew Stone. If it

weren't for his proximity, she could probably muster up a lot of enthusiasm for him as primary suspect in the murder of his ex-wife. Under the circumstances, she didn't want to be convinced of his guilt quite yet, not until they were surrounded by witnesses, at any rate.

"I'm sorry about Lynette," she said, trying a different tack.

He glanced at her skeptically. "Oh, really. You knew her?"

"I'd met her," she said, leaving out how casual that meeting had been. "Recently."

"Must not have talked about me. She could have told you exactly where I was."

"You were in touch?" she asked, surprised.

"Daily." He shrugged again. "One way or another."

"What does that mean?"

"Nothing."

Amanda decided not to pursue that particular line of questioning, though she had a feeling it would have been fascinating. Had he continued his harassment long distance? Instinct told her he wouldn't reveal any more than he wanted her to know, and *nothing* seemed to be it for now.

"How'd you hear about the murder?" she asked.

"Newspapers and TV reach almost all parts of the globe these days," he said as if he were patiently instructing a child that the sky was blue, the grass green, and two plus two equaled four.

"Then you were out of town?"

"Yes, I was out of town," he mimicked.

Amanda had to try very hard to resist the urge to slap the smirk off his face. "In Ohio?"

A tiny flicker in his eyes told her she'd surprised him. He turned away and moved toward the kitchen. His pace was slow and deliberate, as if he'd simply grown bored with humoring her.

From her vantage point a few steps into the dining room, Amanda saw him open the refrigerator and help himself to a soft drink. He passed her on his way back to the living room. She followed, watching as he went straight to a chair across the room. He didn't so much sit down as sprawl, the posture an obvious attempt to affect lazy disinterest in her and her probing questions. His gaze, however, remained alert and suspicious. She decided to allow him to stew a while longer, wondering whose nerves would fray first, his or hers.

"You don't like me much, do you?" he said eventually.

Amanda was startled that his ego permitted such an insight. "I don't need to like you, Mr. Stone. I just need to ask fair questions and write with objectivity."

A smile tugged at the corners of his mouth, and for an instant she could see the attraction he might have held for Lynette. "A polite way of saying you don't like me."

"For a public relations man, you don't do much to make yourself likable," she countered.

"I wasn't aware I was working right now. If you want smooth, practiced charm, I'll stop by next time I'm pushing a client."

"Touché."

"So, what's your angle, Ms. Roberts?"

"I'm investigating Lynette's murder."

"Any luck?"

"Not until you walked in," she admitted candidly.

"Because I'm your chief suspect?"

"Because you can fill in some of the blanks," she corrected. "Tell me what broke up your marriage."

"A difference of opinion."

"About?"

He tilted the can and took a long drink. "What do men and women usually fight about? Love. I was in love with Lynette. She was no longer in love with me, or so she claimed. I think she'd just decided that being married was a nuisance. It interfered with all those little numbers she liked to crunch. When she wasn't analyzing corporate profits and price-earnings ratios, she was training for some marathon. There wasn't a lot of time left for tending to a relationship."

"That made you angry, didn't it?"

"Let's just say it wasn't my idea of marriage, but it was the best she could do. I loved her. I was willing to accept crumbs. Doesn't say much for me, does it?"

"If you wanted to carve out time together, why didn't you run marathons with her?"

"That's not something you do unless you're committed to it. I wasn't. It bored me. It wasn't even conducive to togetherness, not in the way you mean. It's not like you jog along and chat. I'd rather do an hour in the gym and be done with it."

"Who filed for divorce?"

"She did."

"Did you fight it?"

"No. There wouldn't have been any point in a long, drawn-out court battle."

"Maybe not in a court battle, but you did try to change her mind, didn't you?" Amanda said, again recalling the harassment charges leveled against him.

"Constantly," he admitted readily.

"And she called the police."

"Often enough."

"Why didn't you just give up?" she asked, genuinely puzzled. "You're an attractive man. There are thousands of single women in Atlanta."

"Habit. Addiction. Depends on which shrink you talk to, I suppose."

"You saw a shrink?" she asked, suddenly recalling the fact that William Hennessy and his wife had also gone for counseling.

He nodded.

"More than one?"

"No, just the one. Lyn saw another one on her own. She believed in getting a second opinion on everything in life."

"So which one did you see?"

"I've forgotten her name."

Amanda took one more leap, a giant one. "It wouldn't have been Joyce Landers by any chance?" she said, wishing she'd asked William Hennessy the same question. A "yes" from both men would link three of the murder victims—Lauren Blakely, Lynette Rogers, and Landers herself. She watched Stone's face. There was no reaction.

"Could have been," he said.

To Amanda's regret, he actually managed to convey a

lack of recognition without sounding evasive. She waited just in case something else clicked. As she'd expected, eventually he felt a need to fill the silence.

"Like I said, I don't really remember much about the whole experience. Lyn found her, set up the appointment. I didn't buy the crap she was dishing out, so I didn't find her particularly memorable."

"Where was her office?"

He shrugged, his expression vague. "Downtown, one of those towers. I don't recall."

"What did she look like?"

"When Lyn was in a room, do you honestly think I looked at anybody else?"

Amanda sighed. If he knew why she was pushing so hard, it didn't show in his expression. He merely looked annoyed, not distraught or guilty. She wondered if he even remembered that Joyce Landers had been killed. Wouldn't he remember something like that if he'd been in therapy with the woman? She decided to let it go. Maybe it was something Jim Harrison would know, even if he hadn't chosen to share it with her.

While Amanda pondered the possible link, Andrew Stone stared impassively toward the front door. A muscle twitched in his jaw at the sound of two cars pulling into the driveway, the engine of one shutting off. The other car idled, then drove on. His expression bleak, Stone turned toward her.

"They're not going to be happy to see me, you know." Then, with a touch of defiance, he added, "But I have a right to be here, dammit. I loved her every bit as much as they did."

That was the only thing he'd said all morning that Amanda truly believed. In his own odd, twisted way, Andrew Stone probably had loved his ex-wife. But would that have stopped him from killing her if he couldn't have her?

Miriam Rogers was inconsolable. It was all her husband and daughters could do to get the sobbing woman into the house. They were so intent on that, they barely noticed either Amanda or Andrew Stone.

"He cut my baby," she whispered, her voice choked. "How could he do that? How could he cut my baby?"

Amanda recalled what Harrison said about Lynette putting up a struggle. She was the first of the victims to be wounded by the attacker. The others had all been strangled without putting up much resistance.

"Mama, why don't you go upstairs and get some rest?" one of the daughters urged in a soothing tone. "The doctor left some pills. Maybe you should take one."

"No, I don't want pills. What good are pills going to do me? Lynette won't be here when I wake up, will she?" Her voice rose hysterically. "I'll make tea. We could all use a nice cup of tea. Maybe a coconut cake. It was Lynette's favorite." Her voice broke. Her body sagged. Only her husband's quick reflexes kept her from falling. He guided her into the kitchen, trailed by one of Lynette's sisters.

Amanda could feel the woman's pain. It was the kind of raw, uncensored anguish reporters and policemen saw all too often. She'd never been able to harden herself against its chilling effect.

As the sad trio went into the kitchen, the other sisters stood in the doorway to the living room, their gazes shifting from Amanda to their ex-brother-in-law. The venom in those looks seemed about equally divided.

Andrew Stone didn't flinch. He drew himself up out of the chair and squared his shoulders. "Tricia, Jessica."

"You shouldn't be here," said the one he'd addressed as Jessica, her expression judgmental. "It's only going to upset Mama and Papa."

"I came to pay my respects," he said stubbornly.

"We'll tell them," Tricia promised, her attitude more placating. Was she the one always designated to make peace in the family? Amanda wondered.

"Please, Andrew," Tricia continued. "Don't make trouble. They're on the edge as it is."

Amanda thought it was interesting that whatever animosity the two sisters might feel for Andrew Stone, apparently neither feared him. Neither seemed to be accusing him of anything more than insensitivity to their parents' feelings.

His expression grim, his eyes shadowed, he finally nodded. "Did you schedule the services?"

Jessica's mouth firmed stubbornly, but Tricia didn't hesitate. "Saturday at three o'clock at the church. The burial will be after."

"Visiting hours?"

"Tonight and tomorrow night, seven to nine."

He nodded. "I'll be out of there before you arrive, and I'll stay in the background at the services."

Apparently neither woman had the heart to deny him that much.

"Thank you," Tricia said. As he walked past them, she touched his hand. "I'm sorry, Andrew. I know none of this is easy for you, either."

"No," he said quietly. "It's not."

"Mr. Stone," Amanda said, "where will you be staying, in case I need to talk to you again?"

He regarded her evenly. "I have no idea. Guess you'll have to give up the notion of turning me over to the cops."

"I wasn't planning to," she countered. "They're perfectly capable of finding you all on their own."

In fact, she figured they had the entire county staked out by now for just that reason. Knowing what they did about Andrew Stone's obsession with his late wife, the police would have been nincty-nine percent certain that he'd show up for the funeral.

When he'd gone, Amanda looked at the two sisters. Their faces were pale and drawn, their eyes red-rimmed from crying. Even so, there was no mistaking the resemblance to Lynette. They had the same golden coloring, the same crystal blue eyes and sculptured bone structure. The primary differences were in their less sophisticated choice of clothing, their simpler hairstyles. Neither had the same vibrancy, but that could have been due to circumstances, not personalities.

"Could we talk?" she asked them. "I'm sure your father explained about the story I'm doing for *Inside Atlanta*."

"He did," Tricia said cautiously. "What do you want to know?"

"I'd just like you to tell me about your sister, about her friends, what she was like growing up, her marriage. Anything." She told them about her own meeting with

Lynette. "That's why I'm doing the story, because I met her, because she stopped to be kind and perhaps only minutes later she was dead."

Both seemed at a loss to respond to Amanda's question.

"Perhaps we could start with Andrew," she suggested. "Do either of you think he might have been involved?"

"Andrew?" Tricia said skeptically. "Never. He worshiped Lynette."

"But she divorced him."

"It didn't matter. I know the way he felt about her was obsessive. He drove her crazy. She called the police on him. But I don't think she ever was afraid of him, just annoyed because he wouldn't let her go."

"That's right," Jessica agreed, though with a hint of reluctance. "Andrew's not a mean person."

"Yet you both thought his presence here would upset your parents," Amanda reminded them.

"Because they took Lynette's side in everything," Jessica explained. "They automatically figured if she divorced him, then he must have done something terrible."

"Like what?"

Tricia shrugged. "An affair, maybe? I don't know."

"Did they think he was abusive?"

Both women looked genuinely shocked by the suggestion. "Nobody's ever said a word about anything like that. Never," Tricia said.

Amanda switched direction. "Do either of you know anything about the psychologist they went to for marriage counseling?"

"Lynette never talked about any psychologist," Tricia said adamantly.

"Then again, she wouldn't," Jessica added. "Lynette never liked to talk about anything that seemed like failure. I'm surprised she even told us about the divorce. Probably figured she had to, or sooner or later somebody would notice that Andrew wasn't along for holiday dinners."

"Did they only come here for holidays?"

"They came here as little as possible," Jessica said with a trace of bitterness. "Lynette hated it here. She craved excitement, and out here about the most excitement we have are church socials. Papa's done okay with this place. He put us all through college, with a little scholarship help. But by Lynette's standards, he was hardly a success. She loved him and Mama, but she resented the fact that they wouldn't let her help them make a better life for themselves. They were another one of her failures, I guess."

"Did they know how she felt?"

"I doubt it. They loved her. They were proud of her. They were grateful for whatever time she could spare to be with them."

The description reminded Amanda of what Andrew Stone had said. He too had been grateful for whatever crumbs of attention Lynette had been willing to bestow on him. What kind of powerful personality could command such devotion while giving so little in return? Her impression of Lynette Rogers shifted slightly.

She took that insight and applied it to the incident in the park. It lent even more credence to the speculation that Lynette had been at the end of her run. As competitive and driven as she'd been described, it was doubtful she would have stopped to make a kind gesture to a stranger if it would have interfered significantly with her training.

So, if she was to operate on the theory that the killer had known Lynette's habits, that meant someone who'd had an opportunity to observe her on more than one occasion, perhaps even to run with her.

"Did she belong to a running club or something like that?"

Both women shook their heads. "You'd have to check with her friends in Atlanta to find out anything like that."

"Any particular friends you can recall?"

"There was a woman she worked with, Kelsey Hall or Howe. Something like that," Tricia offered. "She mentioned her occasionally. Other than that, she was really a loner. Buried herself in work, then ran to relieve the stress."

"Of course, she did run with Andrew, when they were married," Jessica said.

Amanda fought to hide her astonishment, given Andrew's expressed dislike of running. "Really? Often?"

"That's how they met," Tricia explained. "In the Boston Marathon. Andrew won that year. They ran in the Peachtree Road Race every single Fourth of July weekend that I can remember."

Why had Andrew Stone lied to her? Amanda wondered. Why had he made it seem that running had never appealed to him as much as it had to Lynette? Unless, of course, he hadn't wanted her to guess his familiarity with Lynette's training habits.

"Do you have a picture of Andrew, by any chance? Maybe even a wedding picture?"

"I'm sure there's one in the desk somewhere," Jessica said.

"Could I borrow it? I'll make a copy and get it back to you tomorrow."

"I suppose there's no reason not to loan it to you," Jessica said. Tricia nodded.

The search took only a minute or two, and then Amanda was heading for the door. She could hardly wait to get a copy of the photo into Larry's hands so he could show it to the folks in the park when he ran that night. She wondered if anyone would be able to place Andrew Stone on that jogging path on the night his ex-wife had been murdered.

CHAPTER

Seven

AMANDA screeched to a stop at the first gas station she found with a pay phone. This far from Atlanta she didn't trust her car phone to get good reception. She flipped through her notes for William Hennessy's number. He answered on the first ring, something even a deodorant commercial warned against doing in its *"Never let them see you sweat"* philosophy.

"It's Amanda Roberts, Mr. Hennessy."

"Oh," he said, his voice going flat.

Obviously she'd disappointed him again by not being a prospective client. Or perhaps he simply regretted having been quite so open with her the day before. That happened a lot. She chose to ignore the reaction.

"I forgot to ask yesterday," she said in a way that assumed he'd still be thrilled to cooperate. "What therapist did you and Lauren go to see?"

He hesitated—always a bad sign—then said, "What difference does it make? She can't reveal anything. Patient confidentiality, remember?"

"I wasn't going to question her." If her guess was right, that would be impossible anyway.

"Then why do you need her name?" he asked.

His stubborn refusal just to reveal it and be done with it triggered an alarm in Amanda. "Was it Joyce Landers?" she asked finally, wishing she could see his face as she awaited a response.

"I won't say," he said at last. "Some things are just meant to be private."

Amanda wondered if his reticence was genuinely meant to protect his privacy. Were there things in his record that he didn't want anyone else to see? Was he so uncertain whether confidentiality laws would protect that information that he felt a need to hide even the name of the therapist?

If so, Amanda decided, then the therapist couldn't have been Joyce Landers. He couldn't possibly have feared that a dead woman would reveal his secrets. Or was he simply afraid that the fact of her death linked him to not one, but two murders? Damn! Amanda had hoped that this much, at least, would be simple. William Hennessy had been perfectly straightforward the day before. His attitude now suggested a man with something to conceal.

"If it's a part of the police record, I'll find it out anyway," she reminded him. "You could make my life easier."

"Ms. Roberts, believe it or not, that's not a big goal for me," he said, every last trace of friendliness gone from his voice. "I probably said more than I should have yesterday."

Amanda couldn't recall any incriminating revelations.

She'd have to go over her notes again, though, just to be sure. Before she could try to convince him that he had nothing to fear or to discover who'd convinced him not to talk to her, the phone clicked in her ear.

Annoyed, she punched in Jim Harrison's number. Maybe the detective would be more talkative, especially if she bribed him with a little hint about Andrew Stone's reappearance in the state.

"Miss me?" she said sweetly after he'd growled a greeting.

"Not especially. To what do I owe the honor of this call? Did you run out of other sources to plague?"

"Something like that. I had a conversation with Andrew Stone today."

She heard the front legs of his chair hit the floor with a thud. She had to admit the reaction was satisfying.

"You what? Where? How'd you find him?"

"Exhaustive research," she taunted. It would drive him crazy to think that she'd actually tracked down the suspect first. She saw no need to tell him she'd simply stumbled on the man by accident.

"As it happens, I'm willing to trade that information with you," she added.

"For what?" he said warily.

"Confirmation that both Lauren Blakely and Lynette Rogers had gone to Joyce Landers for therapy."

"Where the hell did you hear that?"

"Is that a yes?"

Dead silence.

"Yoo-hoo, are you there?" she said.

"Yes, Amanda, I'm here."

"Well?"

"Not for publication, not for attribution?"

"Jeez, you don't want much, do you?"

"Those are the terms."

She weighed what she could do with a certain confirmation of that link against the general irritant of giving in to his restrictions. "Okay," she said finally. "Agreed."

"Joyce Landers treated both couples, obviously without much success in the case of the Rogers woman. I do not know this from her records, so there's no confidentiality issue. However, that also means we have no idea what observations she might have had about any of the four people."

"If you haven't seen her records, then how do you know they were patients?"

"Check stubs. Lynette Rogers and Lauren Blakely kept meticulous records. Fortunately for us, neither of them worried about having their therapy discovered. If they'd paid cash, with Stone not around and Hennessy stonewalling us, we might never have discovered the link."

"Any of the others tied to her?"

"Not a one, as far as I can tell. That puts the link one step above coincidence, but a long, long way from anything we can work with."

"Maybe everybody else paid cash."

"I doubt it. And don't forget, Joyce Landers was the second woman killed. Four others came after, including Lynette Rogers."

"So you don't think it's significant?" she said, not bothering to hide her disappointment.

"I don't think it's *insignificant*," he corrected.

"Whatever that means," Amanda grumbled. "Okay, I'll talk to you later."

"Whoa there, Ms. Roberts. Let's not forget about how you earned these revelations. What's the deal with Stone?"

Amanda toyed with telling him everything she knew about Andrew Stone's plans for the next twenty-four hours, but she hated making Harrison's job too easy for him. His brain needed the workout.

"If you're half the detective I think you are, you'll have him by the end of this evening," she said.

"Then you've actually seen him?"

"Yep."

"Amanda, you're trying my patience."

"That's certainly the effect I'm after. Bye-bye, Detective."

She wasn't sure, but the sound she heard as she hung up might have been an exasperated chuckle rather than a curse. Maybe Jim Harrison was finally mellowing.

Upon her return to town Amanda stopped by a copy shop to make a couple of color reproductions of the wedding picture Lynette's family had loaned her. Then she swung by Larry's, hoping he hadn't gone off to see the Braves play. For the first week or two of the baseball season, he was difficult to find anywhere outside of Fulton County Stadium. Once he'd gotten his fix, he seemed satisfied to listen to games on the radio or watch them on cable. It was too soon for that, though.

She flipped on her car radio, then tracked up and down the dial until she found the game. After listening for an inning and a half, she finally heard the announcers mention that the game was being played in Cincinnati. The Braves were winning. Good. Larry would be in a receptive mood when she told him what she had in mind for the two of them that night.

"You and I are going jogging?" Larry said with a note of incredulity when Amanda finally managed to catch his attention between innings.

"Yep. Grab your stuff."

"Now? I thought I was going alone, later."

"Things change. Anyway, it's the top of the ninth," she said reassuringly. "The Braves are winning by five. You won't miss a thing."

He stood up reluctantly. "I suppose we can listen to it in the car," he said as he disappeared into the bedroom to change. It seemed to Amanda that he was dawdling. He didn't turn off the television until they were on their way out the door . . . with two out and no one on base. Only after they were in Amanda's car with the radio on and that last man out did he speak again.

"Now exactly what is it we're going to do?" he asked.

"We're going to show this picture of Lynette and her husband to anyone we see in the park. Maybe somebody will be able to place Andrew Stone on that jogging path Tuesday night. If people follow the same every-other-day regimen Jenny Lee has me on, then the folks who were in the park Tuesday night ought to be back tonight."

"Did you invite Jenny Lee and Donelli along on this excursion?"

"Nope," she said blithely. "Didn't have time. You can

call them from my house while I change. They can meet up with us later."

"I can deal with Jenny Lee, but exactly how am I supposed to calm Joe down when he finds out you're heading back to the scene of the crime less than twenty-four hours after receiving a warning to stay away from this story? He thought I was going alone."

"Then he should be pleased you'll have my protection."

"I doubt it," Larry grumbled.

"Then tell him we'll take my gun," Amanda said in exasperation.

Larry's freckled complexion turned pale. "Oh, no. No guns. I don't believe in them. Do you actually own one?"

Amanda nodded. "The Manhattan police insisted when some indignant bad guys started getting violent after I did a series on judicial corruption in New York. Don't worry. I've got terrific aim. Ask Joe. He watched me wound half a dozen targets at the practice range one day."

"You wounded them? You didn't actually hit any vital organs?"

"I wasn't aiming for vital organs. I aimed to disable them."

"These targets, you mean," Larry said. "You've never actually fired at another human being, right?"

"Haven't had to, thank goodness," she said cheerfully.

Larry grimaced. "Then if it's all the same to you, I think we'll leave the gun out of this."

Amanda smiled. "Whatever you say."

He shook his head. "God, Amanda, sometimes I think you need a keeper."

"Oh, come on, admit it, Larry. Your life didn't begin to get interesting until you met me."

"My life didn't begin to get dangerous until I met you. There's a difference. By the way, did you happen to notice that you are going at least twenty miles an hour over the speed limit?"

She regarded him innocently, then glanced at the dash. "Is that all? I could have sworn I was really pushing this thing."

Larry groaned and buried his face in his hands. He didn't so much as look at her or the speedometer until she'd squealed into her driveway thirty minutes later.

It was just about four forty-five when they reached the park. To Larry's frustration, he hadn't been able to reach either Jenny Lee or Donelli. He'd left messages for both. To Amanda's ear, they had sounded desperate. He didn't seem thrilled with his role as accomplice and protector.

"You go that way and I'll go this way," Amanda suggested. "We'll see more people that way."

"Oh, no, you don't," he said, latching on to her elbow with a surprisingly strong grip. "We go together or I sling you over my shoulder and take you home."

Amanda wasn't convinced he could accomplish that without causing a real scene, but she decided giving in would save a lot of time. "Okay. I figure Lynette was running in this direction the other night."

"Fine. Lead the way."

"But I'll just slow you down. I'm sure you're much faster."

"I'll rein in my urge to sprint by," he said dryly.

The weather wasn't nearly as pleasant as it had been on

Tuesday. It was downright chilly. An earlier storm had left puddles standing on the path. Rain was again threatening. The ominous clouds had kept the families at home. Amanda figured that was going to work to their advantage. Most of those out tonight were dedicated runners who weren't about to let a little rain interfere with their exercise routine. Those were the kind of runners most likely to know a fellow marathoner.

Two men running toward her, their hair damp, their bodies slick with sweat, seemed like a good starting point. She jogged toward them.

"Hi, guys."

They nodded and would have kept on going, but Larry moved into their path. Both men regarded them with a mixture of impatience and suspicion. After checking out Larry's all-American boy looks and Amanda's obvious lack of muscle tone, they relaxed visibly.

"Sorry to stop you," she said, and explained their mission. "Could you look at this picture and tell me if you've seen either of these people before?"

"That's the woman who was killed the other night," said the first, a dark-haired man. "We used to see her almost every time we were here."

"Did you see her on Tuesday?"

The second man shook his head. "Sorry. We weren't here. Our AA group meets on Tuesdays. That's the only night we miss."

"What about the man? Did you ever see him in here with her?"

They glanced at each other and shrugged. "Nope. Sorry. But we just moved to Atlanta about seven months ago. He could have been around before that and we wouldn't know."

"Thanks anyway," Larry said as Amanda fought to hide her disappointment.

When they'd gone, Larry glanced at her. "You didn't actually expect it to be that easy, did you?"

"I always hope it will be," she said dejectedly. As soon as another jogger came into view, though, she perked up and went through the same interview all over again. With the same discouraging results. As the runner took off, Amanda thought she caught a glimpse of someone moving behind the trees.

"Larry, over there," she said, pointing as she instinctively took off across the grass. But just as she reached the spot where she'd noted the movement, she saw a skinny kid racing away in the other direction. She stared after him in puzzlement. "Larry, did that look like Pete?"

"You mean the kid from the other night?"

"Yes."

With his photographer's eye for detail, he stared after the boy. "About the same size and coloring."

"Why would he take off like that?"

"Beats me."

"And what would he be doing back here? You don't suppose he's run away again?"

"Isn't he supposed to visit Joe out at the farm?"

"He said he wanted to."

"I guess you'll have your answer when he calls to arrange it, then."

"I guess so," she said, but it was some time before she could put Pete out of her mind and really concentrate on interviewing joggers again. An hour later it seemed they must have spoken to every runner who'd ventured out. A steady drizzle was falling.

"Maybe we should give it up for tonight," Larry suggested.

"Another half hour," Amanda argued. "It was almost seven o'clock when I saw Lynette. That means she'd probably started sometime after five-thirty or so. Maybe we were just too early."

Two women came along right after that. When Amanda attempted to stop them, they regarded her with obvious wariness. Larry's presence seemed to terrify them.

"Please," Amanda said, falling into step beside them. She introduced herself. "Larry's the free-lance photographer we use. He's helping me out tonight. I'd really like to ask a couple of questions."

"ID," one of them said, slowing slightly.

Fortunately Amanda had tucked her press identification into her pocket. Without breaking stride, the two women studied it carefully, and only after that did they stop.

"Sorry to be so suspicious, but under the circumstances we don't want to take any chances."

"I don't blame you. Actually, that's the story I'm working on. Did you see either of these people in the park on Tuesday night?"

"She's the murder victim," the taller woman said right off.

"And I've seen him," the other said. "You remember, Val, he ran in the Peachtree a couple of times. He tried to pick you up."

"Oh, right," she said. "What was his name? Alex? Alan?"

"Andy?" Amanda supplied.

"Yeah, that's it. This is a wedding picture. Was he married to the woman who was killed?"

"Right."

"Is he a suspect?"

"Only if someone can place him here in the park."

Both women shook their heads.

"But I can believe he did it," said the one named Val. "He really freaked when I turned him down for a date. I was worried he'd follow me at the end of the race, but he didn't, thank God."

So Andrew Stone had a violent temper. Amanda wasn't surprised about that. She'd seen evidence of his barely leashed anger and wondered what it would take to trigger an explosion.

She smiled at the two women. "Thanks. You've been a big help." She handed each a card. "If you remember anything else about Tuesday night, give me a call."

When they'd gone, Larry said, "Face it, Amanda. This is a dead end. Either Andrew Stone wasn't in this park or he kept himself hidden."

As Larry's words sank in, Amanda threw her arms around his neck. "Larry, you're a genius. Come on."

"Come on where?"

"To the spot where Lynette's body was found. Let's see just how good a hiding place it was. If the area provided cover for the killer, maybe it provides cover for some other folks as well."

"You mean the homeless?"

"Exactly."

"Don't you think all the activity would have scared them off by now, assuming there were any there in the first place?"

"From what I've read, once they stake out a territory, they'll go back to it again and again, just as if it were home. they might have stayed away Tuesday because of all the commotion, or even last night, but by now one or two might have ventured back into the area."

"Don't you think the police will have thought of this?"

Amanda shrugged. "Maybe. Maybe not. I'm betting they're not wasting manpower staking it out."

Sure enough, as they crept through the bushes where Lynette's body had been found, Amanda spotted a man wearing a plastic garbage bag like a poncho to protect him against the rain. His clothes, what she could see of them, were filthy, his hair short and unkempt. Hoping not to startle him into fleeing, she eased around a tree until she could approach him from the front.

She opened her mouth to speak, but the greeting died in her throat.

"I wondered how long it would be before you showed up," Jeffrey Dunne said.

C H A P T E R

Eight

"**G**REAT minds think alike, I see," Jeffrey Dunne said, beaming at Amanda as if she'd proved some theory of his. "Hey, Larry. How you doing?"

"Just great," the photographer said, amusement glinting in his eyes. His grin vanished when he caught Amanda scowling at him.

The FBI agent gestured to the damp ground. "Care to join me, Amanda?"

"I don't think so," she replied. "What the devil are you doing here?"

"The same thing you are, I suspect. Hoping a witness will turn up."

"Why you?"

"Short straw. It happens," he said with a shrug. "As you can see, though, I take my assignments, even the lousy ones, seriously. I even dressed for the stakeout."

She had a feeling there was a message in there about her own attitude that Oscar would love. She studied the agent's outfit. Considering his penchant for well-tailored gray suits, button-down shirts, and expensive ties, Amanda figured his current attire must really irritate him.

"And a very attractive outfit it is, too. I especially like the dark green of the plastic. It complements your coloring," she commented. "Any luck out here so far?"

"Not yet. By the way, I like the shorts. Very athletic. What's that in your hand?"

She handed over the photocopy reluctantly.

"Ah, the victim and her ex-husband. How's your luck been going?"

"A lot of people recognize her. Only one knew him, but she didn't see him here on Tuesday night."

"What makes you think he was back in town?"

Amanda weighed her choices—lying, dissembling, or simply telling the truth. She opted for hedging.

"Some of us are blessed with gut instincts," she said with exaggerated modesty. "Well, it's been fun. See you."

"Amanda?"

She paused.

"I don't suppose you'd like to bring me a cup of coffee from that café on the corner?" There was a faintly wistful note in his voice.

She regarded him consideringly. "That would mean you'd owe me one, right?"

"In the overall balance of power, yes," he conceded.

"Then by all means." She glanced at Larry. "You could check out more joggers."

"Oh, I think I'll just amble along with you, if you don't mind," he retorted as Jeffrey Dunne shot him a commiserating look.

Amanda glared at the two of them. "Careful, Agent Dunne. That steaming hot coffee could wind up dumped over your head."

"Why do you give him such a rough time?" Larry asked as they walked to the café. "The guy's just doing his job."

"Blind obedience is not an excuse for what he did to me. He used me, let me worry myself sick that Donelli might be dead, just to solve a case."

"Hasn't he more than made up for that since?"

"How?"

"By not hauling your butt into jail when you stumbled into the middle of a government operation a couple of months ago. He would have been justified. The senior senator from Georgia certainly wanted him to. He managed to avoid it."

"True," Amanda admitted reluctantly. "Look, it's not that he's such a bad guy. We just have different views on the government, on law and order, on journalistic freedom, on just about everything with the possible exception of the color of the sky. I daresay we could probably wind up arguing over that just on general principles."

"Would it kill you to lighten up just a little? It's just possible you could pry a little information out of him, if you didn't always get his back up."

To be honest, that wasn't something that had occurred to Amanda—using Jeffrey Dunne the same way he'd used her, setting him up, pumping him for clues. She tended to be straightforward in her questioning, not sneaky, then found herself irritated when officials remained tight-lipped. The FBI agent was more tight-lipped than most.

Training, no doubt. Maybe it was time to employ another tactic.

"You could be right," she said thoughtfully. She bought Jeffrey Dunne the largest coffee available and a ham-and-cheese sandwich just to start the peace process.

"What's this?" the FBI agent asked when she handed him the sandwich a few minutes later. He took it gingerly and peeked inside the waxed-paper wrapping. "Did you tell them to use spoiled mayonnaise or something?"

"And here I was trying to be nice," Amanda chided. "How long are you going to be on this stakeout?"

"Why?" he asked suspiciously.

Obviously she'd waited a little too long in their relationship to start making nice. "I thought you might want to drop by afterward. Larry, Joe, Jenny Lee, and I will be having dinner. You could join us." She smiled as if the invitation were perfectly natural, as if she hadn't practically thrown him out just the night before.

He studied her curiously. "Are you okay?"

"Fine."

He seemed to be weighing the sincerity of the offer. "I have to hang around here for an hour or two after dark to see if anybody shows up," he said finally. "Don't wait for me to eat. If it's not too late, I'll swing past, see if any lights are on. Maybe you'll save me some dessert."

"Sure," Amanda said agreeably. "See you."

"'Bye, Amanda, Larry."

He still sounded so bemused, it required all Amanda's best efforts to keep from chuckling as they left him sitting there in the rain.

"That was easy," she said to Larry as they left the park.

"You were right. Getting information out of him will be a piece of cake."

"Don't get overconfident," Larry warned. "He agreed to stop by, not to spill his guts."

"Larry, you forget that getting people to spill their guts is what I'm best at doing."

Amanda and Larry made a huge chef's salad from the odds and ends Amanda had in the refrigerator. The lettuce, green peppers, tomatoes, and onions were there courtesy of Jenny Lee, whose eating habits tended to be considerably more healthful than Amanda's. The cheese, sliced ham, hard-boiled eggs, croutons, and fat-laden salad dressing were Amanda's contribution. She figured after that rainy stakeout she owed herself something tastier than the fat-free alternative dressing.

Thinking of her promise to Jeffrey Dunne to come up with dessert, she popped a homemade frozen peach pie into the oven. The previous summer, she had taken a week's vacation at Oscar's insistence and had gone into a rare frenzy of domesticity. The freezer was crammed with peach pies, frozen strawberries, and a couple of berry cobblers. She had even canned peaches for the first time in her life. To her astonishment and Joe's amusement, she had discovered recently that they were actually edible.

Jenny Lee arrived minutes later with a huge round loaf of olive bread from her favorite bakery. Donelli turned up with Bryce Cummings in tow.

"Hope you don't mind," the private investigator said, regarding Amanda with a shy smile. "I ran into Joe earlier today and he invited me along."

"I figured we can always use another perspective," Donelli said.

"Always," Amanda agreed, wondering exactly when she'd learned to like not working entirely alone. "By the way, how'd it go with Pete the other night?"

"His parents were very relieved to see him," Bryce said. "He glared at them and stomped off to his room. I doubt it will be the last time he takes off."

"He called me this morning," Donelli said. "He wanted to come out to the farm. I reminded him it was a school day. We agreed I'd pick him up on Saturday, if he cleared it with his parents."

As he talked, he circled the dining room table, studying the salad and bread with displeasure. "Where's the rest of dinner?"

"This is it," Amanda told him. "There's a pie in the oven for dessert."

He shook his head. "I'll be back."

"Where are you going?"

"We need meat. Start the grill."

"Donelli, we do not need meat."

"We do if you expect my brain to function," he retorted on his way out the door. "I've been planting fields all day. I missed lunch. Rabbit food won't do it."

"I should have know we couldn't pull it off," Amanda said to Larry.

He grinned at her. "It was worth a try. Maybe he'll come back with fish or chicken."

"He said meat. That means steak. Will you start the grill? If we expect any cooperation from him at all tonight, I'd better humor him. Donelli considers only two things to be actual food: pasta and steak. Lettuce leaves do not qualify."

"I'll help with the grill," Bryce offered. "Where is it?"

"Larry, take him out on the deck and show him where I keep everything."

When she and Jenny Lee were alone in the kitchen, Amanda regarded her assistant intently. "Well? Did you find out anything else?"

"I did some more checking on Karl Taylor. This last trip to the drug treatment center was his second. He was sent there the first time about three years ago."

"Who was footing the bills then, Betsy Taylor?"

"Yes. Apparently he had a trust fund, but someone—his parents, I guess—had decided he was incapable of managing the funds himself and had given her power of attorney to dole out the money. He resented the hell out of having to beg her for every dime. She told him if he got help and straightened out his life, she'd relinquish control of his parents' estate."

"So he tried once."

"Right. Apparently he fell off the wagon before she could make any changes. Still, she was willing to stick by the agreement if he went back. He said he wanted to try treatment here again first. When it was clear it wasn't working the second time either, everyone agreed he ought to go back to the treatment center in California."

Amanda's pulse skipped a beat. "Who was the referring doctor?"

Jenny Lee named someone she'd never heard of. "Oh."

Her assistant grinned. "That was this last time. The first

time, he was being treated by . . ." She paused dramatically.

Amanda didn't wait for her to finish. "Joyce Landers."

"Exactly."

CHAPTER
Nine

"**W**HERE'S Karl Taylor now?" Amanda asked Jenny Lee. She reached for her purse and checked to make sure she had notebook, pen, tape recorder, and a satisfactory stash of jelly beans to tide her over until she could get back for dinner.

"He's living at the estate while the will's in probate. Where are you going?" Jenny Lee demanded as Amanda snatched her coat off the back of a chair.

"To have a talk with him."

Jenny Lee groaned. "I should have known. Amanda, you have a houseful of guests."

Amanda had a feeling the reminder was less a comment on her lack of social graces than it was dismay over being left to deal with one particular guest who wasn't going to take kindly to being left behind: Donelli.

Amanda didn't actually have a solution to offer for that particular dilemma. She was sure Jenny Lee could cope.

"Entertain them. I'll slip out the back. They'll never know I've gone," she said blithely, already halfway out the door. "Thanks, Jenny Lee. By the way, Jeffrey Dunne may drop by."

Jenny Lee's eyes widened. For the moment, the announcement had achieved the desired effect. It had distracted her from Donelli's likely reaction to Amanda's abrupt, unchaperoned departure.

"Why?" she asked. "You didn't actually invite him here, did you?"

"I did. Ask Larry. It was his idea. Don't mention any of this stuff about Karl Taylor and Joyce Landers to Dunne, though. He's here so we can pump him for information, not the other way around."

Amanda actually made it all the way to the driveway without being intercepted. She might have completed her escape, if her car hadn't been blocked in by Jenny Lee's. She ran back inside. "Quick, I need your keys. You're blocking me in."

"I'll move the car," Jenny Lee offered.

"There's no time. I'll just take yours."

Jenny Lee paled slightly, but she dutifully turned over the keys. Amanda succeeded in getting back to the driveway and into the recently acquired, sporty little two-seater that was Jenny Lee's pride and joy. She had the engine running and the headlights on before her luck ran out.

A car pulled up, blocking the driveway. Donelli emerged and strolled up. Sighing, Amanda rolled down the window.

"Going someplace?" he inquired.

The casual tone didn't fool Amanda. He was fuming. "I need to check something out."

"In the middle of your own dinner party?"

"It is not a dinner party," she retorted. "It's . . ." Her voice trailed off lamely.

"Well?"

"I do not need to defend myself to you."

"Rudeness is pretty much indefensible."

"I'm working, dammit. Everyone's here for the same reason. We're not here for idle chitchat and a few hands of cards."

"More's the pity."

"Move your car."

"Not until you agree to let me tag along wherever you're going."

"What if I'm just going out to pick up toothpaste?"

"Then I'd say your timing sucks."

His overprotectiveness grated against her independent streak. "Why are you doing this?"

"Amanda, this isn't some political scandal. It's not even an isolated incidence of violence with a complicated web of circumstances surrounding it. We're more than likely dealing with a serial killer who targets young, professional women."

He explained it all with exaggerated patience, while she seethed.

"You are such a woman," he continued in that same slow, careful, immensely irritating tone. "You are also aggressive, smart, and nosy. Those are not traits likely to endear you to the killer. In fact, he has already expressed his displeasure with your journalistic investigation."

He leveled a serious, brown-eyed gaze directly at her. "Just for once will you allow me the pleasure of worrying about you in person, rather than at a distance?"

His quietly insistent plea, combined with is recitation of the very real dangers, cooled her temper almost instantly. "I suppose when you put it that way, it would be foolish of me not to accept your company," she said grudgingly. "Notice I said company, not protection. I do not need protection."

"Are you carrying a gun?"

"No."

"I am," he said calmly. "Did you get around to taking a refresher course in self-defense?"

She scowled at him. "No."

"I did."

"Okay, okay. You've made your point. Move the car and get in."

"I think we'll just take mine."

"Do I get to drive?"

He grinned. "What do you think?"

Amanda moaned. "We will never get there," she accused. Joe observed every posted speed limit with a fanaticism that drove her crazy.

"Do you expect this '*something*' to disappear?"

"I suppose not."

"Good. Then let's do this nice and legal. I'll drop the steaks off inside and we'll hit the road."

While he was gone, Amanda briefly considered trying to maneuver Jenny Lee's car around Donelli's. Unfortunately there would be hell to pay if she got a scratch on either one, and she was already testing her luck with both of them.

In the end, though, that wasn't what stopped her. It was envisioning Lynette Rogers's lifeless form in those bushes, combined with Donelli's common sense warning that this was no time to think of herself as an intrepid loner. For once in her life, it might be wise to travel as part of a pair at the very least. Maybe an entire pack.

Amanda reminded herself to give Jenny Lee the same advice, especially since her assistant had recently begun to demonstrate the same addiction to danger that guided some of Amanda's less wise decisions.

Karl Taylor seemed delighted to see them. Of course, it was clear from the widening of his pupils and his frenetic behavior that he would have been pleased to welcome General Sherman on another march through Atlanta. Amanda wasn't overwhelmed by that sort of indiscriminate, drug-induced exuberance. It could, however, work to her advantage. Karl Taylor was unlikely to have any idea whatsoever what he was revealing, much less to whom.

Tall and thin to the point of emaciation, he had limp blond hair and an aristocratic face. His affected, lord-of-the-manor demeanor was straight out of *Masterpiece Theatre*.

"Right this way. Right this way," he said, lurching ahead of them with an unsteady gait.

In the dark-panelled library, its shelves crammed with rare editions, a fire blazed, even though the damp spring air was hardly cold enough to call for one. The room was oppressively overheated.

"A drink?" he said, waving toward an array of alcohol in crystal decanters.

"No thanks," Amanda said.

"Something else?" He leered suggestively. Amanda

hoped he'd meant to imply an offer of drugs rather than his body, especially since his gaze was directed at Donelli.

"Not a thing," Donelli said, wisely covering all contingencies.

"So, then," he said to Amanda. "You're a reporter." He glanced at Joe. "And you?"

"A friend."

His head bobbed up and down like one of those plastic toys on a spring. "Yes. Yes. Friends who'll trail along on a rainy night are hard to come by. Do you know how lucky you are, Ms. Roberts?"

"Indeed."

"Could you excuse me a minute?" he mumbled, and wandered off.

Hopefully not in search of more cocaine or whatever he was on, Amanda thought.

"The guy's in no condition to talk, Amanda," Donelli said. "I say we split."

"No way. His defenses are down. He'll probably answer anything I ask."

"But will it be the truth?"

"It'll be a start. Besides, do you honestly think he has enough of his wits about him to lie?" she countered just as Taylor returned.

Donelli didn't look overjoyed, but he didn't insist on leaving.

"So, Ms. Roberts, what brings you to see me?" Karl Taylor said after he'd settled onto a leather chair. He drummed his fingers nervously. His gaze darted from her to Donelli and back again.

"I wanted to talk to you about a woman named Joyce Landers," she said bluntly.

Both men gaped at her. Apparently both had figured she'd start out asking questions about Betsy McDaniels Taylor. Donelli was the first to cover his surprise. He simply sank lower onto his own chair and kept his gaze pinned on Karl Taylor.

"What do you want to know about her for?" Taylor inquired petulantly.

"You did know her, right?"

He nodded.

"In her professional capacity?"

He nodded again.

"What did you think of her?"

"You mean as a woman or as a therapist?"

"Both."

"She was attractive, I guess. I didn't really notice. She wasn't the kind of woman who dressed so that you would, you know what I mean? She was sort of subdued like. It was as if she just wanted to blend into the scenery. Probably part of her technique."

"Was she a good therapist?"

He blinked rapidly. "I suppose."

"Was she able to help you?"

"She tried," he said, his voice barely above an agonized whisper.

"How'd you feel when she recommended a drug treatment center?"

"I thought she was wrong."

"But you went?"

"I had no choice," he said bitterly. "They all ganged up on me. Joyce, Betsy, the lawyers."

"So you went to California. Did you continue to resent them for sending you?"

"After a while, once I was clean, I could see that they were right. It wasn't something I could have handled on my own."

"You weren't angry by the time you got back home?"

"No."

"When was that?"

"Last year."

"When last year?" Amanda prodded.

He didn't hesitate. "Spring, mid-April, maybe."

"Could it have been any earlier, maybe even late March?" Joyce Landers had been murdered on April first, April Fool's Day.

He looked as if he were struggling to sort it all out. "No," he said finally. "That couldn't be. When I got back, I wanted to make an appointment with Joyce for a session, but Betsy told me she was dead, that she'd been killed almost two weeks before."

Amanda wasn't entirely convinced. He could easily have come home a week or two before checking in with his family, killed Joyce, then feigned a later arrival. She could probably find out the date of his release from the treatment center or from the police. For the moment, though, she would have to take him at his word.

"When you were seeing Dr. Landers, did you ever meet any of her other patients, maybe in the waiting room or in the hallway as you were leaving?" she asked, thinking of the man the police had considered a suspect.

He shook his head. "She had her office set up to avoid that. Only one client was ever in the waiting room at a time. We left by another door."

"I understand one of her patients was particularly violent, that he used to throw tantrums that were sometimes overheard by clients in the waiting room."

"That wasn't me," he said defensively.

"No, I didn't mean to imply it was. I was just wondering if you ever heard anything like that."

"No. I was usually her first patient in the morning. Most of the time the lights weren't even on when I got there."

"Do you have any idea if she ever held group sessions, say, with people who had similar problems?" Amanda said, wondering if there was any possibility that Lynette Rogers, Lauren Blakely, and their husbands had ever been in such a group together.

He shrugged. "If she did, she never suggested it to me." He regarded her intently. "Why are you so interested in Dr. Landers? I thought you were here to ask about Betsy's murder."

"I'm getting to that," Amanda conceded. "Since you've brought it up, can you tell me what happened? I mean, as much as you know."

He stood up and paced the room, his arms around his middle as if he were trying to keep his body from shivering. When he finally stopped, he chose a place closer to the fire.

"She and I didn't get along," he said straight off. "It wasn't like we were close as kids or anything. Hell, my old man and hers hated each other's guts. It wasn't until my father got sick that he went to Betsy and made the arrangements about the money. If her parents had been alive, it probably wouldn't have happened. He wouldn't have trusted his brother not to steal every penny of the great Taylor fortune. Not that Uncle Richard needed a dime." He gestured around the room. "As you can see, he had done all right here in the family estate, which my father was convinced Uncle Richard had stolen from him."

"But even with all the bad blood, your father put Betsy in charge of your trust fund. Why?"

"Because of the drugs," he admitted openly. "He figured I'd blow it all up my nose. He was probably right." He uttered a dry chuckle. "The hell of it is, I still may pull it off. He's probably turning over in his grave."

"How resentful were you of Betsy?"

"Funny. At first I resented the hell out of her, but the little twit kind of grew on me. She wasn't a bad sort, just a little uptight and naive. The only thing she cared about was that garden of hers. She'd been working out there when she disappeared, plucking weeds with the same care some old harridan would use to tweeze facial hairs."

"You weren't here the morning she vanished?"

"No. I was with a friend. There'd been a party the night before. I wound up staying over. He vouched for me to the police, though I'm not sure how credible either of us was as a witness, given how high we were when they eventually talked to us."

"But you reported Betsy missing?"

"No. It was the housekeeper. When Betsy didn't come down for dinner, Mrs. Lewellyn went looking for her. She found all her gardening tools by the bed of daffodils. She knew right away that something was wrong. Betsy never left those precious tools of hers outside. Mrs. Lewellyn came in, found that my cousin's handbag was still here as well, so she called the police. They didn't talk to me until I wandered in here in the middle of the next afternoon."

"Does Mrs. Lewellyn still work here?"

"No. She retired after Betsy's death. I think she's living with a sister in Florida. The lawyers would know. They send her a check every month."

"Let's get back to Betsy, then. Were you just a little bit relieved when you realized she wouldn't be coming back?" Amanda asked as if it would have been perfectly natural for him to feel that way.

"No," he said adamantly. "You can believe what you want, but like I told the police, I'm sorry about what happened to her. She didn't deserve to be killed. If you ask me, the police never checked out that so-called boyfriend of hers closely enough. I may be all doped up, but I'm harmless. I wasn't so sure about him. I warned Betsy about him, but she was dazzled."

Amanda regarded him in astonishment. Jim Harrison had never mentioned a boyfriend. Had he not known, or had the guy's alibi checked out, taking him off the list of suspects?

"What's his name?"

"Stone. Andrew Stone. Betsy said he'd left town, but I wasn't convinced of that."

Amanda's pulse hammered. Donelli straightened up, clearly as thunderstruck as she was. "And you told the police about him?"

"Sure I did. I guess they figured I was just trying to divert suspicion from myself."

Either that or they were holding a trump card they hadn't thus far revealed to the public.

CHAPTER

Ten

"*T*HAT sneaking, conniving, son of a bitch," Amanda thundered when she and Donelli were finally back on the road.

"Who? Stone? Taylor?"

"No, dammit, Jim Harrison. He never mentioned that Stone was linked to the Taylor case."

"Sweetheart, he is not obligated to give you all his information," Donelli reminded her. "You're lucky he talks to you at all, rather than insisting you go through the official Atlanta PD spokesman. There are lots of reasons why a cop wouldn't share everything he knows about a case with a reporter."

"I'm not just any reporter."

He glanced at her, a wry expression in his eyes. "For purposes of this discussion, let's just say that all journalists are equal in the eyes of a policeman trying to do his job."

Amanda wasn't wild about being lumped in with average beat reporters and TV newscasters looking for nothing more than a ten-second sound bite. "Okay, let's say I concede the point, with some reluctance. Name one reason he'd hide such an obvious connection between two cases. Isn't that obstruction of justice or something?"

Donelli actually chuckled at that. "No, Amanda. It's obstruction of justice when you do it. It's smart detective work when he does it. Releasing that information prematurely might jeopardize the investigation. Harrison might not want it bandied about that Andrew Stone is tied to two cases until he has sufficient proof to take to court. He might not want the guy skipping town."

"Again," she reminded him. "Stone has been in Ohio, remember?"

"We don't even have solid evidence of that. The rumor was that he vanished. The trail led to Ohio, but we don't have confirmation that he actually went there or, if he did, that he didn't turn right around and come back here months ago. You heard Taylor say that his cousin swore that Stone was gone, but he didn't believe it."

Amanda dismissed the technicality with a wave of her hand. "All I know is that Saturday at Lynette's funeral I am going to have a little talk with Andrew Stone myself."

"And ask him what? If he was fooling around with Betsy Taylor, while he was supposedly trying to salvage his marriage to Lynette?"

"That's just for starters."

"You met the guy today. Did you get any indication that he would be likely to tell you the truth, especially if it implicated him in a murder?"

She glared at Donelli because neither the elusive Stone nor the sneaky Detective Harrison was available. "No."

"Then settle down and let's see what that Ohio DMV check of mine turns up in the morning. I have a friend at Delta, too. Maybe he'll check airlines records for me. Maybe then you'll have some hard evidence about Stone's comings and goings in and out of Georgia."

Amanda started to argue, then sighed. "Thank you."

"For what?"

"For allowing me to blow off steam. For keeping me from steamrolling over a possible suspect and ruining whatever chance there might be to catch him in a lie."

He grinned at her. "I consider it my civic duty. Besides, I like you on this side of prison walls, not inside, which is where Harrison would be likely to ship you if you mess up his investigation."

"Any particular reason?"

He glanced over. The raw desire in his eyes—a desire he'd banked for months now while she sorted through her emotions—said it all.

"None you're ready to hear quite yet," he said quietly.

Amanda sighed and laid her hand on his thigh, which tensed beneath her touch. "Not quite," she agreed.

But the days of resisting the way she felt about this man were definitely nearing an end. When they had first met, they had been drawn together by a rare intellectual compatibility that had been shaken but not destroyed by this rough patch in their emotional lives. With each day that passed, the bond strengthened as she let him back into her life. His patience counterpointed her impulsiveness. His logic nicely balanced her impetuosity. His strength was a more than even match for her own. Now, more and more, it was their physical intimacy that she missed with something akin to an ache. But both of them recognized that this time the relationship required a total commitment. She wouldn't go back to him until she could make it.

Back at the house, Jenny Lee and Larry were entertaining a still scruffy-looking Jeffrey Dunne. There was no sign of Bryce Cummings.

"Where'd he go?" Donelli asked.

"He said he was working a surveillance. He left right after Jeff showed up," Jenny Lee said. "He seems like a nice guy. How do you know him, Joe?"

"We met while he was still with the Atlanta police. He wasn't much for taking orders. Had one too many blowups with his supervisor, and they suggested he might be happier in another line of work."

"How'd he get a license as a private investigator with that on his record?"

"He really didn't have any black marks against him, except for insubordination. He actually was a damned good investigator. This seems to have worked out best all around. Did he say anything about what he was working on?"

"Not a word," Larry said.

Donelli shrugged. "Doesn't surprise me. He was always pretty tight-lipped. Actually, it's a good quality in a PI."

Amanda scowled at him. "Depends on which side of the fence you're on. I could use a couple of sources right now who have an urge to talk." She glanced hopefully at the FBI agent.

"Don't look at me," Jeffrey Dunne said. "The peach pie was great, but it's not enough to get me to release confidential information."

"So, you do know something," Amanda said, sitting down beside him. She reached for the pie plate and waved it under his nose. "More pie?"

"I've had two pieces."

"Oh. How about a drink? Maybe a nice brandy?"

His lips twitched with amusement. "I don't think so."

Amanda's gaze narrowed. "Did you find a witness in the park tonight?"

His innocent expression never wavered. "Nope."

"Have you got the FBI profilers working on these cases?"

"Me personally?"

"You, your boss, some bozo in Washington," Amanda snapped impatiently. "I'm not particular about who started it. I just want to know if it's happening."

"They didn't consult me about anything like that."

"You're still skirting the question, dammit."

He nodded. "Yes, I am."

Amanda ignored the amused chuckles from her supposed friends. Obviously she lacked the necessary finesse to pull this off. She glared at the FBI agent. "You are a very frustrating man."

He winked. "Thank you."

Ready to make one last-ditch try, she rose and ambled toward the kitchen. At the doorway she glanced over her shoulder, rather seductively, she thought. "And here I was willing to tell you where you could find Andrew Stone."

Jeffrey Dunne moved with amazing speed for a man wearing unlaced shoes at least three sizes too big. "Now, how the hell would you know a thing like that?" he asked.

"It pays to be in the right place at the right time," she informed him airily.

"And what place was that?"

"I can't quite seem to recall."

"Amanda," he muttered.

His fists clenched as if he were fighting the urge to strangle her with his bare hands. She'd seen the gesture frequently enough to recognize it. "Yes, Jeffrey," she said sweetly.

"Tell me exactly where and when you saw Andrew Stone or I will haul you down to headquarters and let my meanest, nastiest colleague cross-examine you from now until next weekend."

Given the fact that he wasn't smiling when he made the threat, Amanda took him seriously. Given that she wanted very much to be at that funeral on Saturday, she said, "How about a trade?"

"Let's see how much I think your information is worth and then we'll talk about it," he countered.

"That's not a trade. You could renege."

He smiled. "I know. I guess you'll just have to trust me."

Donelli, Jenny Lee, and Larry were observing the bargaining as if they'd wandered into a high-stakes poker game.

"Trust you?" Amanda repeated as if the concept were not only alien to her, but preposterous given their past history. "Now why would I want to do that?"

"Because you don't have much of a choice," Dunne suggested.

She glanced at her watch and made a decision. She

would throw him a bone. "Andrew Stone was planning to be at the funeral home before official visiting hours started tonight."

Dunne chuckled. "That's it? That's all you have? That was hours ago."

His derision irked her. "He'll be at the funeral."

"Where is he now?"

That, of course, was what Amanda herself wanted to know. She wouldn't mind taking another crack at interviewing him before all these other clowns took their official shots. Unfortunately she didn't have a clue.

"Sorry," she taunted, as if she knew but just wasn't telling. "You have to give me something to prove good faith."

She held her breath as he seemed to weight the challenge.

"I suppose I could suggest you might want to pop in at the police station first thing in the morning."

Her gaze narrowed. "What are you saying?"

"Just that your pal Jim Harrison has hauled in the man who might have been responsible for killing Marnie Evans. After letting him stew overnight in a cell, I'd say the interrogation ought to get interesting by morning."

"The mysterious lawn man?"

"That's the one. A guy by the name of Martin Luther Washington."

"Why aren't you down there?"

"I wasn't invited."

Amanda decided not to wait until morning. She grabbed her coat and purse on her way to the door.

Donelli regarded her with a look of resignation. "And

here I thought we were all set to play a friendly game of poker."

She grinned. "We just did. I won."

Jeffrey Dunne was still sputtering with indignation as she took off.

Amanda felt better than she had in months.

C h a p t e r

Eleven

SHE should have waited until morning. Martin Luther Washington was locked up tight. Jim Harrison was off doing something that no one seemed inclined to share with her. Exasperated, Amanda went home, caught a few hours of sleep, and dragged herself back to the station just before noon.

This time she had better luck.

Martin Luther Washington, if that's who it was seated across from Jim Harrison in the glassed-in cubicle, was a thin black man wearing a yellowed T-shirt and jeans that were covered with grass stains. With his huge brown eyes darting around the station and his knee jerking to some silent rhythm, he looked scared out of his wits.

"Help you, miss?" asked a passing policeman.

Amanda shook her head. "I see the person I need."

He followed the direction of her gaze. "You mean the detective?"

"Nope, the man with him."

"Yeah, I hear he's a suspect in one of those murders. Washington or something?"

"Martin Luther Washington," Amanda suggested.

"Right. Just go over and tap on the door. Doesn't look like much is going on. They've been sitting there glaring at each other for the past hour."

Amanda approached the cubicle and beamed a friendly smile at the suspect. His gaze locked on her as if she'd arrived with a pint of whiskey and bail money. Her favorite detective didn't look nearly as excited to see her.

"You a lawyer?" the black man asked anxiously when she'd stepped into the room and closed the door.

Amanda shook her head. "A reporter."

His shoulders sagged. "I was hoping maybe you was the one they sent to get me out of here."

She glanced at Jim Harrison. "I don't suppose I could maybe sit in while you and Mr. Washington talk." She sounded more humble than usual in the hope Harrison would be shocked into compliance.

"Sure. Have a seat," he said magnanimously.

She regarded him with suspicion. "It's okay?"

"Sure, why not?" he said. "Of course, you won't be in on much of a conversation. Mr. Washington has declined to discuss much more than his name until he gets an attorney."

The man cast a belligerent glare at Harrison. "Don't see why I should. I have rights, same as anybody else. You ain't gonna pin that lady's murder on me. No way. She paid me like always that Friday and I left. That was that."

"So, why'd you make it so tough for us to find you, if you were innocent?" the detective demanded.

"You gonna take my word, just like that?" he said with a derisive sniff. "No, sir, I don't think so. I just took me a little trip. Went to visit my mama over to Alabama. Came back day before yesterday."

"Why'd you come back if you knew you were under suspicion?" Amanda asked.

"Tired of listening to her complaining. Remembered why I left home in the first place. Besides, I figured it would all have blowed over by now." He shot a look of disgust at Harrison. "Thought you cops were smart enough to solve this thing and let me go on about my business."

With the comment delivered as insultingly as possible, he folded his arms across his thin chest in a defiant gesture. "And that's all I'm saying."

The silence dragged on. Amanda didn't doubt for a minute that it could go on indefinitely. They'd clearly reached an impasse. Judging from how exhausted they appeared to be, pretty soon they'd all be snoring from the boredom of it. She glanced at Jim Harrison. "Could I speak to you in private?"

He shot an impatient scowl at his suspect, then nodded. "Might's well." He called over another officer to keep an eye on Washington.

Outside the cubicle, he led Amanda to the coffee machine, where sludge was being dispensed. Amanda looked at it and shuddered. "Surely you don't intend to drink that?"

"How do you think I keep my wits so sharp?" he retorted. "Drinking this stuff is like mainlining caffeine. Drink enough and you never need sleep."

"Unfortunately, it doesn't quite cover the exhaustion or

the need for a shave. What kind of hours have you been putting in, Detective?"

"Nonstop," he admitted. "I want this case solved. I don't sleep well anyway when there's some sicko out there murdering young women."

"Maybe you'd do better if you took a few hours off to relax, maybe mull over what you do know. You keep pushing and your brain will short-circuit."

"You let me worry about my brain," he retorted without much spunk. He yawned. "By the way, I heard you stopped by in the middle of the night. Who tipped you that Mr. Washington was down here?"

"Maybe I just got lucky."

"And I'm J. Edgar Hoover."

"Be glad you're not," she retorted. "So, Detective, how about letting me talk to him?"

"Not a chance."

She offered up her most charming smile, even though she knew Harrison was immune to her wiles. When he let her in on things, it was always because he had an ulterior motive.

"Come on," she urged. "What have you got to lose? It's not like he's spilling his heart out to you."

He glowered at the reminder. "What makes you think he'll talk to you?"

"Because he's indignant. He thinks he's being wronged by the justice system. He'll probably be more than happy to pour out all his complaints to a sympathetic ear, especially if said ear doesn't have the power to lock him away for a slip of the tongue. The thought of sharing his views with *Inside Atlanta*'s readers will probably be the most exciting opportunity ever to come his way."

"I think you're overestimating your readership, Amanda. I doubt our friend in there has ever heard of the magazine. My guess would be he opts for the supermarket tabloids."

"Just wait 'til I flash my business card at him and wow him with circulation numbers. He'll be convinced it would be a disservice to the citizenry of Atlanta not to talk to me."

Harrison didn't look convinced. He finished off the coffee and crumpled the cup, tossing it toward a trash can. It missed. "Typical," he muttered. He looked at Amanda. "You gonna let me listen to the tape?"

"Not if it was a hundred and ten and you were holding my feet to a fire."

His expression brightened. "An interesting thought. But if I don't hear the tape, what's in this for me?"

"The vague hope that I'll pass along any pertinent revelations."

"You have an odd way of bargaining, Amanda. You get everything you want. I get hope."

"Life isn't fair," she conceded. "But right now you've been at it for hours and you don't even have hope."

"How am I supposed to explain this access to a suspect, when the rest of the media gets wind of it?"

"I work for a monthly magazine, remember? By the time my story comes out, the access should be pretty well equalized. It won't be a problem."

He looked too tired for further argument. "Fifteen minutes. If that attorney shows up sooner, you're out. Agreed?"

"Agreed."

When she returned alone, Martin Luther Washington

regarded her suspiciously. "What do you want?" he asked, keeping a wary gaze on Harrison and the other officer, who were now out of hearing distance, though still within view.

As Amanda followed the direction of his gaze, a third man she recognized walked up and joined them: Bryce Cummings. He must be there working on the case he'd mentioned at the house the night before, she thought. Or maybe he was just visiting his old cronies. She shrugged it off and turned her attention to the man seated across from her.

"If what you're saying about Marnie Evans being alive when you left her is true—"

"It is true," he interrupted vehemently.

"Okay," she soothed. She wanted him agitated, but at the system, not at her. "Then it sounds to me like you're getting a raw deal. Maybe I can help. I'm trying to find out who killed her and whether it's linked to the other women who've been killed. Maybe you saw something that day, heard something that would point my investigation in a different direction."

She was careful to differentiate between her own snooping and that of the police. She hoped he understood the subtle difference. Judging from the alarm that sprang instantly into his eyes, he didn't.

"You saying they think I killed all them women, not just the doc?"

"I don't know what the police think, but even you have to admit there's certainly a strong possibility that the cases are linked."

"I didn't even know them other women," he swore. His

hand curled into a fist. He pounded it against his knee. "Never saw 'em. I wasn't even here the last three or four months."

"That's right. So let's back up a little. How long had you worked for Dr. Evans?"

With his brow furrowed, he seemed to be weighing whether or not to answer. "Couple of months," he said finally. "Ever since I got out of jail."

"Jail?"

"Drunk and disorderly."

"Did you serve much time?"

"Nah. They tacked on a battery charge just because I bloodied the guy's nose, then kept me inside a couple of weeks to make a point. Soon as my trial came up, they let me go with time served. With no priors, they have a hard time justifying wasting a cell on a guy like me."

"What did you do for Dr. Evans?"

"Cut the grass, pulled weeds, cleaned up the leaves. She had one of them big old oaks. No matter how clean I got that yard, it was covered with more leaves the next week." He shook his head sorrowfully. "I was gonna put in a vegetable garden in the back for her this spring. She was really looking forward to them tomatoes."

"How'd you happen to get the job?"

"Springtime and fall I go around knocking on doors. Most folks have a little extra work getting the yards ready for summer or cleaning up all them leaves in the fall. I've got my own mower and one of them leaf-blower things I wear on my back. Works like a charm. Get 'em all piled up, then bag 'em for the garbage pickup. Carry all my stuff around in the back of my truck."

"You have regular customers?"

"Couple of dozen, maybe more. I could give you names. They got no complaints about my work. I gave those names to the doc. Don't know if she checked 'em out. She hired me straight out. Looked me up and down, then said I had the job. They lady was okay. Paid in cash."

"You ever go in the house?"

"Never. Not once."

"How come they found your prints on a glass inside?" she asked, expecting an angry, defensive denial. He didn't bat an eye.

"It was hot that last day. Indian summer, I suppose you'd call it," he explained, leaning forward earnestly. "She brought me out a glass of ice water, that fizzy kind they sell in them fancy green bottles. French, I think it is."

"Perrier?"

"That's the one. Told her tap water would have been just fine, but I was much obliged. I took the bottle and the glass to the back door when I went for my pay."

Amanda wondered what had happened to the bottle. Probably no one had thought to go through the garbage. The glass must have been sitting on the counter or in the sink, maybe even in the dishwasher.

"Tell me about Dr. Evans."

He regarded her blankly. "What you asking me to say? I didn't hardly know the woman."

"I'm just asking for an impression. Was she friendly, uppity, mean?"

"Naw, she was a real pretty little thing. Had those big eyes. Reminded me of the way Little Red Riding Hood must've looked when she spotted that wolf in Grandma's clothes. Kinda surprised. She always asked how I was doing, then listened real close like the answer mattered to her. Guess that was because she was a doc, huh?"

"Maybe," Amanda agreed. "Or maybe she was just the kind of person who cared about people."

"You listen real good, too," he said awkwardly, clearly uncomfortable with dishing out compliments.

"That's my job. Now think back to that day, Mr. Washington. Was she alone when you went to get your money?"

"Far as I know. I didn't see nobody inside, leastways not in the kitchen. Looked to me like she was getting ready to cook dinner, though. She ate real healthy like. Lots of vegetables, fruit, things like that. That's why she was so interested in that garden I was gonna put in. We talked about it all the time. She'd show me some of them seed catalogs and ask what I thought."

He paused thoughtfully. "Come to think of it, though, she did have an awful lot of food out. Might have been some chicken or fish. Never saw her fix that for herself."

"Any strange cars in the driveway or on the street?"

"Lots of 'em on the street around there. No way to tell if any belonged to somebody visiting the doc."

"What was her mood?"

"No different than usual. She was a real upbeat type of person."

"How was she dressed?"

"I don't recall. A dress, maybe. Nothing fancy, if that's what you're asking." Again, he hesitated.

"What?" Amanda said. "What did you remember?"

"It just occurred to me that she had on perfume, something that smelled mighty fine. I remember now teasing her about it, saying she must be expecting somebody special."

"What'd she say?"

"Just that she had some kind of business appointment, then a friend was coming over for dinner."

"Any names? Come on, Mr. Washington. Think back. Did she say a friend was coming by or did she say So-and-so, maybe John or Ted or Larry?" She deliberately didn't mention Andrew. She didn't want to be responsible for planting an idea in his head.

For what seemed an eternity he wrestled with the question. "Near as I can recall, ma'am, she never said a name. I'm real sorry."

"That's okay," Amanda said with a sigh. Jim Harrison already knew who the date was. That's who had reported the murder. It hadn't been Andrew Stone. But Stone could have been the business appointment, perhaps. Maybe the doctors had hired a public relations person to market their family practice.

She patted Martin Luther Washington's rough hand. "Thanks. You've been a big help." She handed him a business card. "If anything else comes to mind, give me a call."

The minute she was out the door, Jim Harrison was in her face, yet another cup of that disgusting coffee in hand. "Well?"

"Not much." She regarded him intently. "Was that Bryce Cummings I saw with you a few minutes ago?"

"Yeah. You know him?"

"Joe brought him by the house a couple of times."

"He's a solid investigator. He drops in here occasionally. I pick his brain. He's the one who alerted me that Washington was back in town."

"How'd he know?"

"A little unofficial surveillance, I suppose. So what's the deal with Washington, anyway? You get anything out of him? You had a couple of hours with the guy."

She glanced at her watch. The time had definitely flown. "Where the hell's the guy's attorney?"

"Held up in court. Come on, Amanda, what did he give you?"

"Just an idea, actually. Did you find the doctor's appointment book for that day?"

"I think so. If you're thinking she'd written in a meeting or something around the time of the murder, you can forget it. Her last patient was seen at the clinic at three. Her date, one Hank Morton, arrived at six-thirty. He had an airtight alibi up until the minute he walked in. There wasn't a blessed thing on the book in between."

"But Morton was on her calendar?"

He shook his head. "No. Why?"

"Don't you think she would have made a note of the date?"

"Hell, I don't know how the woman thought. Maybe she kept all her personal stuff in her head."

"No. A professional woman with a schedule as chaotic as Marnie Evans's must have been would write down everything. Maybe she did keep her personal schedule on another calendar, though. Did you look for one in her purse or around the house?"

He scowled at her. "If there had been a calendar, we would have found it."

"You were there for the search yourself?"

"Part of the time," he conceded. "The evidence techs did the search."

"You wouldn't want to take a look around the place again, would you?"

"Now?"

"I'm wide awake," she told him. "And you look wired enough to go dancing."

"Sorry, I can't leave our friend in there."

"To bad," she said, sighing with exaggerated disappointment. "See you, Detective."

She actually made it all the way to the door before a voice echoed across the room.

"Oh, Amanda."

She glanced back.

"Go home. Have a nice dinner. Get a good night's sleep," he advised. "I'd hate to have the officer doing surveillance over there tonight haul you in here for breaking and entering."

She tried to work up a little gratitude for the warning, but all she could manage was irritation. She considered looking for a neighbor with a key, But even if somebody on the block had one, it was doubtful she could sweet-talk her way inside Marnie Evans's house under the watchful eye of some cop.

She stopped for a hamburger and some decently brewed coffee. Then, once it was dark and just in case Harrison had made up the surveillance threat, she drove past the modest little house with its neat yard and wrought-iron fence. Sure enough, there wasn't a cop or anyone else in sight.

Cursing the detective again for his sneakiness, Amanda parked around the corner and strolled down the block. Still there was no sign of anyone observing the house or her activities, with the possible exception of a couple of neighbors whose curtains seemed to drop back into place when she glanced their way.

She eased through the front gate, then circled the house, hoping to find a window cracked or even a door left ajar. Unfortunately the place was locked up tight.

Disgusted, she made her way to the back door, which was sheltered from view. She had one hand on the knob and with the other was trying to jimmy the lock when she heard a faint whisper of sound. She froze in place as her stomach began to churn.

Just as she was about to dive for the bushes, she heard a muttered curse, and a familiar hand latched on to her elbow and spun her around.

Given a choice between humiliation at getting caught and righteous outrage, she went for the latter.

"Dammit, Joe Donelli, you almost scared the living daylights out of me! What the hell are you doing sneaking around here after dark?"

"I had this odd call from a detective I know. He suggested that if I was missing the woman in my life, I could probably find her lurking in the bushes trying to break into a house. He suggested I get her before the police did." He glared at her. "Naturally I said that what he was suggesting was impossible, because the ethical reporter I know doesn't break into places. He laughed, Amanda."

She winced at the condemnation in his voice. They had had this discussion before. He didn't approve of her unorthodox methods of gathering information. It was too bad he'd caught her at it.

"There could be important evidence in there that could break these murder cases wide open."

"A fact that you obviously mentioned to Jim Harrison."

She nodded. "He couldn't get away."

"And naturally you couldn't wait for some nice, legal search by the police to unearth said evidence?"

"I never claimed patience as one of my virtues." She lifted her gaze and met his, hoping he would heed the appeal in her eyes. "Just a little peek?"

"Not a chance. Let's go, Amanda."

With one last, longing look at the back door, she went. "Damn Jim Harrison," she muttered.

"He saved your sorry hide," Donelli reminded her. "He didn't have to send me over here after you. He could have dispatched a cop."

"Why doesn't that cheer me up?"

"Beats me. Come on," he said, guiding her toward his car.

"I have mine," she reminded him. Maybe if he left, she could circle around and come right back.

If the grip he had on her arm was anything to judge by, the same idea had occurred to Donelli.

"We'll just leave yours right here," he said in that pleasant little voice that grated on her nerves.

"How am I supposed to get it?"

"I'll bring you back in the morning."

Donelli staying over at her house? An intriguing notion.

"You'll bring me back?" she repeated, just to make sure she'd understood correctly.

"That's right . . . when we meet Detective Harrison to take a walk through the house."

Amanda's mood brightened considerably. The next few hours definitely held some interesting possibilities.

Twelve

DONELLI'S decision to sleep on the sofa in her office had left Amanda incredibly irritable. She hadn't exactly invited him back into her bed, but during the drive home, she'd rather hoped that the decision was going to be taken out of her hands. Instead, it seemed, he was waiting for her to commit to making an honest man out of him.

She scowled at him over coffee, taking slim satisfaction from the fact that he seemed to have a stiff neck from trying to scrunch his tall frame onto her short sofa.

"Care for an aspirin?" she inquired nonchalantly.

He glowered at her. "No. Dammit, Amanda, did it ever occur to you to get a bed for the guest room?"

"No bed, no company. I learned my lesson when my mother practically moved in a few months back. I left the spare bed behind. Besides, that's my office."

"Floor-to-ceiling boxes, a hard sofa that must have done duty in some general's office in World War One, and a computer still in its factory box do not constitute an office."

She regarded him with curiosity. "Why are we arguing about this?"

He hesitated. "Because we're sublimating," he said finally with a faintly sheepish grin.

"You mean we're both cranky because we didn't have sex last night."

"Or the night before that or the night before that." He regarded her intently. "Unless I'm mistaken and you've been sneaking off to Paris with that arrogant, devious Frenchman."

So Oscar had blabbed, Amanda thought. Good. Seeing Donelli jealous was doing a lot to improve her mood. "Armand did suggest Paris," she admitted. "He called again just the other day."

Joe's gaze narrowed. "You going?"

"I've thought about it."

"And?"

"And I'm waiting for a counteroffer."

"You want him to throw in Bordeaux and the French Riviera?"

The predatory glint in his eye was very satisfying. Any second now, Amanda decided, he was going to explode and haul her up from the chair by the kitchen table—or maybe throw her down on top of that cluttered table—and demonstrate why a trip to anyplace with Armand LeConte was not in the cards.

"I have always wanted to go to the French Riviera," she confessed casually.

His gaze darkened. "Amanda . . ."

"Yes, Joe."

"You are not going anywhere with Armand LeConte." He bit out the order.

She regarded him innocently. "Oh? Why is that?"

"Because you and I are going to get married," he announced, his furious gaze daring her to contradict him. He started to pace.

"Soon," he added. Three strides took him to the sink. He made a U-turn. Three more brought him back to the table, where he towered over her. "We'll do it the minute we can get a license. No more games. No more delays. We both know that no matter how furious we've been at each other, no matter how disillusioned, the bottom line is that we love each other. We can work out the rest if we take it one day at a time." He scowled at her. "Well? Aren't you going to say anything?"

"I didn't hear a question."

"Can we reschedule the damned wedding or not?"

She could feel the grin spreading across her face, the relief washing through her. "Well, when you put it like that, so romantically and all, how could I possibly refuse?"

He opened his mouth as if he were prepared to argue. Then he blinked. "Was that a yes?"

"It was."

His own grin matched hers. "Well, hallelujah!"

Now he hauled her to her feet. And swept everything off the kitchen table onto the floor. And then he started to remind her of exactly how much she would have missed if they hadn't ended this terrible stalemate in their personal relationship.

"Hey, Donelli," Amanda said when she could finally catch her breath an hour or so later, "this table is even harder than that sofa. And you weigh a ton."

"Now who's being unromantic?" he chided, but he scooped her up and headed for the bedroom.

Unfortunately, on the way they passed a clock. It was eight-fifteen.

"Ohmigosh," she murmured. "Put me down."

"Why? Surely you aren't suddenly concerned about straining my back?"

"We were supposed to meet Harrison fifteen minutes ago."

"I'll call and explain," he promised. "In a little while."

"No, we have to get into that house."

"*You* have to get into that house," he corrected with an air of resignation. "I would be perfectly content to remain in this house."

"Would you really? When you're expecting Pete to come visit this morning?"

Now it was Donelli's turn to mutter a curse. "Let's go. I'll drop you off at the Evans house and head on out to the farm."

They made it across town in record time by Joe's standards. He actually ran one yellow light. Amanda was proud of him. Maybe he was just anxious to get rid of her and rethink his impulsive decision to push for a wedding.

When they reached the doctor's place, Jim Harrison was sitting behind the wheel of his car, sound asleep.

"You gonna wake him?" Donelli asked.

"If I want to get into that house and still make the funeral, I'd better. You go on."

She opened the car door, only to have Donelli snag her arm and drag her back for one last kiss. "We have plans to make," he reminded her, eliminating any worries she might have had about him having second thoughts.

"I'll stop by on my way back from the funeral," she promised.

The slamming of the car door woke the detective. He blinked and stared at her. "How long have I been out of it?"

"That depends on when you got here. It's a little after nine."

"You're late," he accused.

"And aren't you glad? That's probably the most sleep you've had lately. Have you been inside?"

"Nope. I thought I'd wait for you."

"I don't see a For Sale sign. I'm surprised her family hasn't gotten rid of this place long before now."

"She has a brother who's still debating whether or not he wants to sell. He's in real estate over in North Carolina. He figures the market for this place will improve once people forget about the murder. In the meantime, he's left it as is. Says neither he nor his parents can stand the thought of coming over here to clear out her things."

Amanda could understand that, but she also knew that not doing it would keep them from reaching some sort of closure.

Inside the house, Harrison gave her free rein to explore. "Just don't touch anything. Call me if you find anything you want to check out more closely."

"And where will you be? Catching a few more winks on the victim's sofa?"

"No, Amanda," he said with exaggerated patience. "I will be checking out other rooms."

Ignoring the sarcastic retort, Amanda headed for the kitchen, the room where Marnie Evans's body had been found. There was still a chalk outline on the shining linoleum. Pots and pans sat on the stove much as she must have left them. A meat cleaver sat on the counter, reminding her that the killer hadn't resorted to wounding his victims until Lynette Rogers had struggled with him. That readily available cleaver could have made quick work of the job, but he hadn't touched it. Instead he'd strangled her.

What was the significance of that? Amanda wondered. Was it symptomatic of a man who merely wanted to silence his victims by choking off words rather than breath? Had their deaths been almost an innocent aftermath of that symbolic silencing? If so, what would a psychologist have to say about such a killer? Had he done something he wanted no one to tell? None of the victims had been sexually assaulted, so that wasn't it. Some of the victims were in a position to know secrets—a lawyer, a doctor, a psychotherapist—but the others? A stockbroker, an heiress, and an architect. It was doubtful they would know anyone's darkest secrets.

Amanda sighed. She needed to know a lot more than she knew now if she were to figure out the psychological implications. For now she could concentrate only on finding the appointment calendar that she absolutely knew Marnie Evans must have kept with her at all times. Where, though? An office? By one of the phones? In her purse?

She started with the counter beneath the wall phone in the kitchen. There was a yellow Post-it notepad there, a handful of pens, several menus from nearby restaurants that delivered. There was even a small calendar from an insurance company, but it wasn't the kind with space for noting appointments. Nor was there any sign of her handbag in the kitchen.

Amanda moved on to the living room. The furnishings were sparse, as if she hadn't had time to settle in. Her taste ran toward Early American, not unlike the furniture Lynette Rogers's family owned. Everything was neat as a pin, except for a fine layer of dust that had no doubt accumulated in the months since the murder.

She finally located the phone on a small, rickety table behind a chair. Again, there was a notepad beside it, this one from a pharmaceutical company. Apparently it was brand new, because she couldn't even spot any indentation from a pervious notation. Again, no handbag. Nor was there an address book.

She met Harrison as she was climbing the stairs. "Anything?"

He shook his head.

"Was her purse taken into headquarters?"

"No. As a matter of fact, that's one of the reasons we thought it might have been robbery, because there was no sign of her purse or credit cards."

"Washington told me she paid him in cash. She must have had it in the kitchen with her, but I can't find it, either. Have the credit cards been used?"

"Nope. And the companies have all been notified to

call us if anyone tried to use them. They're recorded in the computers as stolen."

"Damn," she muttered. "This doesn't make sense."

"I still say it's possible that Washington killed her, took whatever cash she had on hand. It could have been a lot, if she'd been to the bank to get money for the weekend."

"But why wouldn't he go through the house and take jewelry, any other small valuables, while he was at it? Was anything missing?"

"No," he admitted. "I just double-checked the jewelry box upstairs. Not that she had a lot or that I'm any expert, but there were a couple of obviously expensive pieces. Maybe the thief just didn't want to risk being in the house any longer than necessary."

"What about a watch? Was she wearing one?"

"Yes," he conceded grudgingly. "A Rolex, in fact."

"Surely he would have taken that. He wouldn't have had to budge from the kitchen to get it."

"Unless the date came to the front door and scared him off."

"Possible certainly, but I think you're really reaching here. Do you like this guy as a suspect for some particular reason you haven't mentioned?" Amanda asked.

Harrison sighed wearily. "No. I'd just like to solve one of these cases. Prove that they're coincidence, after all." He regarded her with a bleak expression. "Any ideas? You're a woman. If that purse was in the house, where would she put it?"

Amanda tried to envision the sort of life-style Marnie Evans would have led, hectic, fast-paced, always on the run.

"If I were the doctor," she said slowly, "I wonder if I would even carry a purse. I could lock it away, but what if I had to leave the office in a hurry to get to the hospital for an emergency? I sure wouldn't carry one on rounds."

Suddenly she thought of the bulging pockets she'd seen on doctor's lab coats, pockets that were stuffed with notes, prescription pads, pens, maybe even a wallet.

"Her lab coat," she said. "Have you seen it?"

His eyes brightened with instant comprehension. "Upstairs. Behind the bathroom door, I think. Or maybe it was in the bedroom."

He took the stairs two at a time, with Amanda right behind him. Sure enough, the white coat was draped across a chair. One pocket was jammed with slips of paper, mostly notes on patients, plus a couple of yellow Bic pens missing their caps. The other contained one of those compact but thick weekly planners, one for the previous year. It was bound in leather and obviously well used.

Amanda reached for it automatically, then glanced at the detective.

"Go for it."

With trembling fingers, she opened the clasp. A twenty-dollar bill fell out, along with a gasoline credit card. Amanda paid no attention to them as she hurriedly flipped through the pages, looking for the right week in October. She ignored the slips of paper and business cards, intent on finding the critical date of Marnie Evans's murder. Each page contained surprisingly neat entries given the penchant most physicians had for indecipherable scrawls.

"Almost there," she murmured as she came to the first week of the month. Anticipation rising, she flipped the page—and came to the third week. Disappointment spread through her as she looked at the detective's expectant expression. "It's not here."

"What do you mean it's not there?"

"The page with the date of Marnie Evans's death is missing. Whoever killed her must have taken it."

CHAPTER

Thirteen

All the way to Lynette Rogers's funeral Amanda tried to figure out what kind of appointment Marnie Evans would have had the day she died. Obviously it could have been almost anything, a workman servicing the furnace, a plumber fixing a clogged drain, Andrew Stone to discuss PR for the family practice partnership. She kept coming back to Stone, probably because she'd disliked him on sight. Hardly the sort of objectivity required of a journalist, she chided herself.

Who would know for sure, though? The doctor's colleagues at the practice? Hank Morton? He might not be a bad starting point. Maybe she could get a fix on him at the same time. Airtight alibi or not, he was the one person besides Washington everyone agreed had been in Marnie's house that afternoon or evening around the time of her death.

Using her car phone, she called information and found a number for a Henry Morton. It was the closest the operator could find to anyone named Hank. Amanda dialed, hoping she might luck out and find him at home late on a Saturday morning.

"Yo, Morton here," an answering machine reported. "Well, actually, as you can tell, I'm not here in person, but I will be sooner or later, and I'd sure like to talk to you. Do your thing at the beep."

He sounded young enough and loose enough to be the Hank Morton she was looking for. Frustrated, Amanda hung up. She didn't want to leave a message. It would put the ball in his court, and she always, always preferred to keep it in her own. Besides, she had no way of telling if it really was the right man.

Which brought her back to Andrew Stone and how she might get him to admit whether or not he'd ever had any contact with the doctor. She certainly doubted he'd ever been a patient. He looked disgustingly healthy and arrogant enough to believe he'd always be that way. No, it was more likely that the doctor had seen him in his professional capacity.

There was one other way she might be able to check that out before she saw him. She called information again for the listing for Marnie Evans's partners, praying they would have Saturday office hours. In a family medical practice, wouldn't that be a necessity to accommodate working parents and school-age kids?

When a cheerful receptionist named Susie answered, Amanda identified herself. "I'm sorry to bother you, but I have a couple of quick questions I'd like to ask one of the doctors."

"They're all with patients right now. I could have one call back."

"Maybe you can help me. Do you know if the doctors have ever considered doing a little marketing?"

"You mean like advertising?" she said a bit more cautiously. "Did you want them to take an ad in the magazine?"

"No. I was just wondering if they might have talked to a public relations expert at some point, tried to find new ways to attract patients."

The receptionist laughed. "I can't imagine why they'd do that. This place is like a zoo every day as it is, but I can check. I've only been here a month. Maybe they did something before I came that would explain this chaos."

"I'll give you my car phone number. It's really important that you have the first doctor available give me a call. I'm about to interview someone, and it would be helpful if I had this information first."

"I'll do what I can," she promised.

Ten minutes later the car phone rang. Amanda snatched it up.

"Yes."

"This is Dr. Nate Williamson," announced a harried voice. "I had a message to call you."

"Yes, Doctor. I'm doing a story for *Inside Atlanta* about the murders of the six young women. I'm trying to discover if they might be linked."

"I thought that was a given."

"Not yet."

"If it'll end this uncertainty about Marnie, how can I help?"

"I was wondering if you and your partners ever considered hiring a marketing person to help promote the practice."

Just as the receptionist had earlier, he laughed. "Not a chance. The last thing we need are more patients. We're working sixteen hours a day as it is. If you happen to know another family medicine doctor or two, though, we sure could use them."

"Sorry," Amanda said. "Do you know anything about the man Marnie Evans was supposed to have a date with the night she died?"

"Hank Morton?"

"Yes."

"Sure, I know Hank. He plays basketball with a group of us every Sunday morning. Good guy. Easygoing. Midthirties. Marnie's death really shook him up. Not that they had anything hot and heavy going as far as I know, but they were good friends. Discovering her body changed him. I don't think he's gotten over it yet."

"Do you have any idea where he works?"

"We're a pretty casual bunch. Other than my wife and I getting together for a beer once with Marnie and Hank, the rest of us don't socialize much off the court. I think he's in advertising, public relations, something like that. When you asked about the marketing earlier, I thought maybe you were thinking about him."

"No," Amanda admitted. "One last question. Do you have any idea what kind of business appointment Dr. Evans might have had the afternoon she was killed?"

"Not a clue. You might call my wife, though. She and Marnie were close, though I believe she told the police everything she could remember." He gave her his wife's number at the hospital, where she was head nurse in an ICU unit.

"Thanks, Dr. Williamson. You have my number if anything else comes to mind."

Just as she hung up, Amanda reached the church where the funeral service was scheduled. The parking lot was already filled to overflowing. She found a space down the block, debated for a minute, then called Terry Williamson, praying that the reception would hold for the call.

Just as her husband had earlier, the nurse sounded harried until Amanda explained the story she was working on. Then she said briskly, "What can I do to help?"

"I'm told Marnie had a business appointment the afternoon she was killed. Do you have any idea at all what that might have been about?"

Amanda sensed Terry Williamson's hesitation. "It's really important," she prodded. "If you know anything, it might help."

"Marnie had been seeing someone . . ."

"Hank Morton," Amanda said.

"No. I mean they saw each other, but he wasn't the problem."

"Problem?"

"Yeah. This guy she'd met at some professional meeting, another doctor, I assume, though she never said that. He wouldn't let her alone."

"Was she frightened of him?"

The question drew a chuckle. "Marnie wasn't frightened of anything. She would have taken on Sherman's army single-handedly with a shotgun without batting an eye. But she didn't like being harassed. She'd made up her mind to do something about it."

"What did she intend to do?" Amanda asked, envisioning Marnie confronting this guy in her kitchen, confident she could handle him, only to have him turn on her.

"I'm not really sure. I warned her to be careful, that the guy might not be as harmless as he seemed, but she shrugged off the warning."

"You told the police about the guy?"

"Absolutely. Unfortunately, she'd never mentioned his name. It was as if she were almost superstitious about talking about him, as if saying his name would make him too real. Crazy, huh?"

"But she did know his name?"

"I'm pretty sure she did."

"Is there any way she might have invited Hank Morton over that night to help her deal with the jerk?"

"I doubt it. She was too independent to ask anyone to help her out of a jam. Whatever she had in mind, it was something she intended to handle herself."

Amanda thanked her, hung up the phone, and tried to figure out how what she'd been told fit in with the other murders. It came back to Stone again.

Had he been there not for business, but to hit on her? He wasn't a doctor, but he might have attended some medical meeting to drum up business. And he did have a certain reputation with women. Hadn't one of those joggers she and Larry had met in the park mentioned that he'd tried to pick her up at a race? On top of that, he'd insinuated himself into Betsy Taylor's life, even though he'd still been married to Lynette at the time.

But how the hell was she supposed to prove that he'd been in Marnie Evans's house that day? Or that he even knew her?

The most obvious and direct way, the one she preferred, was simply to ask him. Trusting him to tell the truth was another matter entirely.

She slid out of her car, locked the door, turned toward the church—and stopped dead in her tracks. It looked as if her opportunity were going to come sooner rather than later.

Andrew Stone was standing off to one side, largely ignored by the members of Lynette's family, who were surrounded by friends. Mr. Rogers looked bewildered but stoic. Mrs. Rogers looked as if she might go to pieces again at any second. Tricia, Jessica, and the third sister stood by her protectively. All three appeared worried. At least twice, Tricia glanced toward Andrew, her expression sympathetic. Her gaze skittered away almost instantly as if she feared anyone noticing, Andrew included.

Amanda observed them from a distance, waiting until the family walked into the church before joining Andrew Stone. He regarded her indifferently.

"Mind if I ask you a question?" she asked.

"Now?"

"Unless you'd like to go for coffee after the service."

He shot a rueful look toward a couple of inconspicuous men posted just inside the front door of the church. "I doubt I'll have time afterward," he noted.

Amanda recognized a couple of cops when she saw them and suspected he was right. They were there to keep an eye on him through the funeral, then to haul him in for questioning. She was almost surprised they hadn't caught up with him at the funeral home on one of the previous two evenings. Obviously he'd been as careful to elude them as he had been to avoid Mr. and Mrs. Rogers.

"Then let me ask now," she said. "Did you ever go out with Marnie Evans?"

He regarded her with a blank look that appeared genuine. "Who?"

"A doctor," Amanda explained succinctly, not wanting to get caught up in the question of present or past tense.

"Sorry. Never heard of her."

"How about Betsy Taylor?"

There was a flicker of something in his eyes at that, but he shrugged it off by reminding her that she'd said she had only one question.

"Never mind. I think you've already answered the second one as well."

He stepped toward her, closing in on her space in a way that was confining even outside on the wide-open lawn of the church. "Don't ever, ever make assumptions about me, sugar."

The low warning might have left her trembling if it hadn't infuriated her so. She really hated being warned off of a story by some creep who was clearly up to his eyeballs in the middle of it. And she really disliked being called "sugar" by anyone.

"Is that a threat?" she inquired quietly, shooting a pointed look in the direction of the nearby policemen who were observing the two of them with interest.

He smiled as if it had been a huge joke. "Yes," he said cheerfully. "It was."

Then he turned and walked away. To her surprise, she wasn't nearly as frightened as she probably ought to have been. Either her gut was telling her something she didn't want to hear about Andrew Stone's innocence or the presence of those policemen had made her complacent.

Amanda followed Stone into the church. As she passed the undercover policemen, one said, "Trouble, Ms. Roberts?"

"Nothing I can't handle," she said as much to reassure herself as to forestall having them rush to her rescue. She wanted all of them—the police, Andrew Stone, and herself—to play this scene out to its end.

She glanced around the crowded, overheated chapel, wondering if Lynette's friend Kelsey was there. Today might be a good day to speak to her. As she surveyed the mourners, she spotted Stone seated in the very last pew and off to the side. He was unobtrusive, just as he'd promised Tricia he would be. She couldn't seem to look away.

As the choir's hymn soared through the old church and sunlight streamed through the stained-glass windows, Amanda thought she saw his cheeks glisten with the dampness of his tears. It softened her attitude toward him ever so slightly. Then she reminded herself sternly that even the worst criminals had friends and family members they genuinely loved.

The service was emotional and long, the eulogies so stirring that Amanda felt her own eyes repeatedly filling with tears. When it was over, Stone slipped out of the pew and made his way to the door ahead of the throng. The cops approached him, but he said something and they backed off, though not by much.

Amanda lingered as well, as close as she dared, wondering if he was merely waiting for Lynette's casket to be carried to the waiting hearse or if there was another reason he'd insisted on remaining longer.

She had her answer when two men joined him, exchanged a few words with him, and then left. It was an innocent incident under the circumstances. Sympathetic words were being murmured all around. Only in this instance, Amanda realized with a sense of astonishment that she recognized both men.

One was Donelli's pal Bryce Cummings. The other was Hank Morton, whose picture she'd seen in one of the newspaper articles about Marnie Evans's murder.

Aside from the fact that their presence at Lynette Rogers's funeral was unexpected, their friendliness with Stone was also a stunner. Not an hour earlier Stone had denied having any idea who Marnie Evans was. Was that possible, if he and her best buddy Hank Morton were even casually acquainted? Doubtful. More likely, Andrew Stone had blatantly lied.

But why, unless he felt the noose squeezing more and more tightly around his neck?

CHAPTER

Fourteen

AS soon as she recovered from the shock of seeing Andrew Stone, Bryce Cummings, and Hank Morton chatting so cozily, Amanda glanced around for Tricia or Jessica, hoping they could point out Lynette's friend. She spotted Tricia staring at Stone as he was discreetly escorted off by the police. She walked over and joined her.

"Tricia?"

The young woman, her eyes red-rimmed from crying, regarded her blankly at first, then with nervous recognition. "I really have to join my family," she said quickly.

"I won't keep you. I was just wondering if Kelsey was here, Lynette's friend from work?"

Looking relieved that Amanda's question was that innocuous, Tricia nodded. "I saw her earlier." She looked around at the mourners still clustered on the lawn, then pointed to three women. "Over there. She's the one in the apricot-colored suit with the long black hair."

Still keeping her eye on Bryce Cummings and Hank

Morton, Amanda made a quick dash toward Kelsey and introduced herself. "It's Kelsey Howe, right?"

"Hall," the woman said.

"I'm in a rush right now, but I wonder if I could call you later this weekend. I'd like to talk about Lynette for an article I'm doing."

The slender, dark-haired woman nodded. "I'll be happy to tell you whatever I can. She was a wonderful friend." She jotted her number on the back of one of Amanda's cards and handed it back to her.

The minute she had Kelsey's promise of an interview, Amanda took off toward the parking lot. She caught up with Cummings and Morton beside a snazzy red sports car Amanda would have killed to own.

Bryce nodded. "Hey, Amanda. I figured I'd run into you down here."

"You never mentioned you knew Lynette," she said.

"I'm sorry to say I didn't. I've been working a case. I had to trail somebody down here."

"Not me, I hope," Hank Morton said jokingly.

Bryce smiled. "No. Not you."

Amanda introduced herself to Morton, since Bryce didn't seem inclined to do it. "Actually, I've been looking for you. I wonder if you have a few minutes now. I passed a burger place on the way to the church. We could get a cup of coffee."

"A few minutes?"

"I promise."

He glanced at Bryce. "You want to tag along?"

"Nope. I've got to get back to my case. Good to see you, Amanda."

She knew better than to ask what case he was working. If he was anything like Joe, he wouldn't divulge anything. Too bad, too, because she sure wanted to know why a private investigator had followed somebody to Lynette's funeral. She kept her mouth shut, though, and waved as he took off in a dull gray car that was perfect for stakeouts and tailing people unobtrusively.

When he was gone, she glanced longingly at the red car, which had probably set the owner back more than her yearly salary. "Yours?" she asked Morton.

He grinned at her, clearly thrilled with his possession and delighted that she appreciated it. "Isn't it a beauty? I swore one day I'd own one of these. I figured I better get it out of my system before I got married. Not a lot of room for kids." He gestured toward the passenger door. "I could drive us over to the burger place, bring you back after."

The temptation was too great to resist. If the man was a murderer, at least she'd go after riding in her own dream car. She cast one wistful look toward the driver's side.

"No way, Ms. Roberts," he said, obviously guessing the direction of her thoughts.

She sighed. "I don't blame you."

For a man with a car that could probably travel faster than light, Hank Morton drove as if there were a cop on his back bumper. It required every ounce of restraint Amanda possessed to keep from reaching across and jamming his accelerator foot to the floor. She figured that would be a lousy way to get a source to cooperate. She took the time to study him. He looked to be about thirty. His clothes were expensive. She'd seen an ad for the tie recently. Eighty-five dollars from some Italian designer whose name she couldn't pronounce. Add that up with the car and it was obvious that Hank Morton was far more successful in the PR business than Andrew Stone had reportedly been.

All too soon, they reached the tiny hamburger place with its hand-lettered sign and jukebox music blaring through the open front door. Maybe, Amanda thought wistfully, she could get him to detour onto the highway and open it up on the way back to the church.

Inside the restaurant, the smell of grease and home-baked pies was too much for her. Instead of coffee, she ordered a burger, fries, a large soft drink, and a piece of the blackberry pie she'd seen displayed on the counter.

"I missed lunch," she explained. "Order whatever you like. I'm buying."

He stuck with coffee, which was probably why he looked as trim as an athlete. A runner, perhaps?

"How'd you know Lynette?" she asked when their order had been served.

"Actually I'd only met her once or twice."

"Then why'd you drive all the way down here for the funeral?"

"Courtesy," he explained. "A gesture for a colleague."

"Oh?"

"Andy Stone and I worked together a couple of years ago."

The news didn't stun her, but it certainly suggested that Andy Stone had lied. Wouldn't he and Morton have discussed Marnie Evans at some point, even if Stone hadn't met her?

"For how long?" she asked, hoping to establish exactly how well acquainted the two men had been.

"Six, maybe eight months. Not long. He left the firm."

"And you've stayed in touch?"

"Not really, but we were friends back then. I felt I owed it to him to show up today. Why all the questions about Andy?"

"I spoke with him right before the service. I asked him if he knew Marnie Evans. He said he didn't. Any idea why he'd deny something like that, if the two of you were friends?"

Hank Morton didn't bat an eye. "Sure. I hadn't even met Marnie myself when Andy and I worked together. If they knew each other, it would be news to me, too."

After a much too brief flare of hope, Amanda's spirits sank. She tried not to let it show. She didn't want him calling his old buddy and reporting her fascination with his activities. "Let's go back to the day of Marnie's murder, then. Tell me what happened."

For an instant Hank Morton looked as if he'd rather be someplace else, discussing almost anything but the day on which his friend was murdered. Finally he swallowed hard and began to speak.

"We were going to have dinner. I got there about six-thirty. Marnie's car was in the driveway, but she didn't answer the door. I thought at first she might be in the shower or something. I walked around to the back. She didn't always lock that door the way she should. When I got there, the door was ajar. I pushed it open." His eyes clouded over then, as if he could still see the terrible scene. "She was . . . she was on the floor."

"Did you see any sign of the gardener the police think might have been involved?"

"No. No one was around."

"The police told me you have an alibi right up until the time you arrived at her house. Mind telling me what that is?"

He shrugged. "Why not? I was in a dentist's chair having my teeth cleaned. Believe me, the way I hate that, you can bet I knew exactly what time I got into that chair and what time I got out again. I left there exactly fifteen minutes before I got to Marnie's. Police records show my call came in about two minutes after that."

"Dr. Evans reportedly had an appointment scheduled earlier. Do you know anything about that? Who it might have been with? If it had anything to do with the man who'd been harassing her?"

His eyes widened. "You know about that?"

"I just heard about it today. I was wondering if she'd invited him over to settle things and he turned on her."

"I suppose that's possible. She was tired of being victimized and too stubborn to let anyone else help her. I'd tried to get her to call the police, but she wouldn't do it."

"Did she ever talk about the guy, tell you who he was?"

"Not a word. She just said he was some creep." He paused, suddenly thoughtful. "You know, she did mention that she was about to turn the tables on him."

"Any idea what that meant?"

"Not exactly, but wouldn't it make sense that she meant to start harassing him in some way? Maybe she found out something about him and intended to use it against him."

From what she'd heard of Marnie Evans's determination to handle her own problems, to be in control of her own life, that sounded exactly like something she might do. But that still left Amanda without any way to identify this man, short of going door to door at every hospital and clinic in town, trying to locate a mysterious physician with a penchant for harassment. And if it hadn't been a doctor, but someone in some related profession, well, the possibilities were too extensive even to begin to contemplate a search.

Amanda ate the last bite of her pie as she debated what she should do next. At some point, she realized that Hank Morton was studying her intently. She had to admit she found the gleam of fascination in his eyes flattering, if untimely.

"You busy tonight?" he asked.

She nodded. "Sorry. I'm having dinner with my fiancé to discuss wedding plans."

He took the news in stride. "Too bad. I miss having someone who'll listen the way Marnie did. You're a lot like her. My hunch is you're just as independent, stubborn, and tenacious as she was."

"So my friends tell me," she said just as she heard the distant sound of her beeper from the bottom of her purse. She fumbled until she found it, checked the calling number, and excused herself. "I have to call my office. Do you mind waiting a minute?"

"Nope. I'll take care of the bill."

"No. This is on me." She pulled a twenty from her purse and tried to hand it to him. He waved it off.

"It's been my pleasure. Besides, I'll owe you if you can

discover what really happened to Marnie. I'm still not sleeping well at night."

Amanda squeezed his shoulder sympathetically as she passed by on her way to the phone.

"Okay, Oscar, what's all the commotion about?" she demanded when she had him on the line. "I'm in the middle of an interview."

"The commotion is that I want you back in this office as fast as that car of yours will get you here. I'm pulling you off the story."

Amanda nearly dropped the phone. She tightened her fingers around the receiver. "Excuse me?" she said softly.

"We'll discuss it when you get here."

"We'll discuss it now."

"No, we won't," he said, and slammed down the phone to emphasize the point.

She stood there in shock for a full minute, then turned and practically ran through the restaurant. "Let's go," she told her startled source. "I have to get back to Atlanta immediately."

He didn't waste time arguing. Only after they reached the car did he look over at her and comment, "You're obviously upset. Has something happened?"

"Yes. I think it's entirely possible that my editor has lost his mind. If he hasn't, then I am about to quit my job."

Amanda tore out of the elevator, raced past the startled receptionist, and headed straight for Oscar's office. She didn't even slow down when she saw that he was in conference with Jim Harrison and Jeffrey Dunne. They looked mighty absorbed in the discussion. They also looked as if they might be about to present a united front. It didn't bode well for her.

"What the hell is this all about?" she demanded.

Oscar didn't bat an eye at her fury. She considered that another bad sign. He usually began to waver once he had to deal with her outrage in person.

"It's about this," he said, handing over a sheet of computer paper that had obviously been printed out of the *Inside Atlanta* system.

Amanda read the threat. It was much like the one Jeffrey Dunne had delivered to the house. She shrugged.

"So what? We knew the guy wasn't going to be happy. This isn't the first time he's warned me to back off."

Oscar turned red. "Yes, so I hear. That is something you and I will discuss after these gentlemen leave."

Deeply regretting the slip even though they'd already spilled the beans, she ignored the barely leashed anger in his voice. "Let's not overreact. How'd this get into our system? Where'd you find it?"

"In my file," Oscar said. "If you ask me, that's one step too close to having him hand-deliver it to you."

"Okay, let's settle down a minute," Jeffrey Dunne said, trying to inject a note of calm into the tense atmosphere. "Amanda, obviously you've been stirring up a hornet's nest that even the police hadn't disturbed. Why don't you tell us what you've been up to?"

"You want me to tell you about my investigation?" she said incredulously. She looked to Oscar for support. He didn't seem inclined to offer it.

"We could subpoena your notes," Dunne reminded her.

"You wouldn't get them," she retorted. "And you know it."

"But it might be fun to try," he countered. "And all that time in court would slow you down, don't you think?"

She glared at him. "You can be such a smug bastard."

"It's a talent I've had time to perfect since knowing you."

"Now, children," Jim Harrison soothed, trying to smother a laugh.

Both Amanda and Jeffrey Dunne glared at him. He wasn't fazed.

"Amanda, look, I understand your reluctance to part with information, but we're all on the same side here," Harrison said.

She scowled at him. "Not exactly."

"We all want to solve these murders, right?"

She could hardly disagree with that. "True."

"If you have something we should be following up on, would it be so unethical to share it?"

She sighed. "Look, if I had any idea what had triggered this guy's response, I would tell you . . . probably. But I haven't talked to anyone you haven't spoken to. I'm still just as much in the dark as you guys," she said, though she practically choked on the admission.

"That's not what the killer thinks," Oscar pointed out.

"Maybe we should forget about who you've talked to specifically," Dunne suggested. "Let's look at the connections. Have you found anything at all linking these cases together?"

She decided to relent . . . up to a point. "There's an Andrew Stone link to several, even indirectly to Marnie

Evans through Hank Morton. I don't know much about the lawyer yet. I was planning to start digging into Daria Winters's background next. I wanted to talk to that guy who blamed her for his being in jail."

"We've talked to him," Harrison said.

"So have we," Dunne added. "It's a dead end."

"Maybe so, but I want to get a better picture of what she was like. I need to talk to some people who knew her." She glanced at Oscar. "Am I on this story or not?"

"I don't like it, Amanda. I've got a real bad feeling about it." He studied her worriedly. "If I pull you, will you back off?"

"I think you already know the answer to that."

He sighed heavily. "Damn, I hate this. If anything happens to you, it'll be on my conscience until the day I die."

"Nothing is going to happen," she said confidently. "I'll start carrying my gun, if that'll make you feel better."

"Why does that make me cringe?" Dunne said.

"Afraid I'll turn it on you?" she inquired sweetly. "I'm licensed, and believe it or not, I'm a decent shot."

"You'd better be better than that," Jim Harrison warned. "I'll take you to the practice range myself."

The door opened just in time for Donelli to hear that last remark. "I'll take her," he said resignedly. "Maybe this time I can get her to aim at something higher than a foot."

CHAPTER

Fifteen

AMANDA didn't like the way the gun felt in her hand—the weight of it, the cold metal, the inherent deadliness. She didn't like aiming it straight at a man's heart, even if the man was no more than a featureless flat target on a practice range. Like it or not, she squeezed the trigger and fired.

Donelli lifted the protective gear over her ears. "Again," he said.

With some reluctance she fired again, saw the bullet rip through the target, and flinched.

"Again."

Her arms were quivering from the tense, outstretched gripping of the gun. "Joe, that's enough," she protested. "If that guy's not dead by now, he's not going to be."

He glared at her. "Again, Amanda."

Because she wanted to get off the practice range and back into her investigation, she fired off two more shots in quick succession, hitting almost exactly the same spot. Deadly aim, if she did say so herself.

Donelli squeezed her shoulder. "Okay. Enough," he mouthed, the words silenced by the earmuffs.

She removed the protective devices, turned them in, and then followed him out and back to his car.

"Not bad," he conceded once he was behind the wheel and they were headed back to *Inside Atlanta*.

"What do you mean, 'not bad'?" she asked indignantly. "Those bullets practically went through the same damned hole. I told you I hit exactly what I aim at. By the way, how come you turned up at *Inside Atlanta* when you did? I expected you to be tied up showing Pete around the farm all day."

He frowned. "Pete never called."

Amanda was surprised. The kid had taken an obvious liking to Donelli—to both of them, for that matter. "Do you suppose his father wouldn't let him come out?"

Donelli shrugged. "I have no idea. I'll check into it later. Maybe give him a call to see how he's doing. I just hope the kid hasn't taken off again."

Amanda shared his concern. "Speaking of calls, you didn't answer me before. Did Oscar call you about the note in the computer?"

His grip on the steering wheel tightened ever so slightly, just enough to be perceptible to someone looking for bad signs. Amanda caught it immediately. He also seemed extraordinarily intent on his driving, which might have been understandable if they hadn't been stopped at a light.

"Not exactly," he said.

"Jenny Lee?"

"No."

She regarded him closely. He looked very uncomfortable. "I'm not going to like the answer, am I?"

He glanced over, then back at the traffic light. "Probably not."

"Try me."

He met her gaze evenly then. Whatever uneasiness he was feeling, it was apparently nothing compared to his conviction that what he'd done was right. That made Amanda more wary than ever. Donelli's "end justifies the means" value system occasionally butted headlong into her own more liberal beliefs.

"After that first note, I hired somebody to keep an eye on you," he admitted.

"You what?" Outrage made her blood pound. "Why the hell would you do that?"

Suddenly she recalled bumping into Bryce Cummings at the funeral, the mysterious case he'd mentioned. "Let me guess. Bryce Cummings."

Donelli nodded. "Sorry," he said, not actually sounding the least bit apologetic. "I was worried. I knew you'd never let me tag along playing bodyguard, so I did what I thought I had to. I told him to maintain a low profile, but I wanted him around if anyone started making moves in your direction."

On the one hand, the gesture was rather sweet. On the other, it rankled, as a testament to his lack of faith in her ability to outwit the killer. "I do not need a bodyguard," she said, emphasizing each word.

"I am not the first man to think you did," he reminded her. "That Frenchman had one of his goons follow you all the way down here from Virginia when you started dabbling in international intrigue. Miss Martha hired her nephew to look after you when you got tangled up with the KKK."

The latter had probably been the most humiliating moment of Amanda's entire life, especially when she realized that Miss Martha's nephew was a pediatrician, albeit one who lifted weights in his spare time.

"I wasn't thrilled with them, either," she snapped at Donelli. She tried to bring her temper under control. Logic would get her farther than yelling. "Look, occasionally your work as a private eye is going to get you into sticky situations. How are you going to feel if I start hiring protection for you?"

"It's not the same."

"Yes, it is."

"Amanda, I am not impetuous. You are. I do not think I'm invulnerable. You do. And I do not seem to irritate nearly as many people as you do."

"I'll take that as a compliment on my reporting skills," she said.

"I was afraid of that."

"Will you call him off?"

"Will you let me take his place?"

"No."

"Then I can't call him off. This story's not the same as the others. You not only fit the profile of the previous victims, but the killer has flat-out warned you that you're next in line. He's warned you twice, if I understood what was going on in Oscar's office just now. Have you taken any precautions whatsoever?"

"I'm carrying my damned gun."

"Under duress. Look, I won't ask you to drop the investigation, but I would never forgive myself if you were out there on your own and something happened."

She wanted to object, but as much as she hated admitting any vulnerability, she could understand his reasoning. And he wasn't asking her to stop reporting the story, only to take sensible precautions. It might grate, but she supposed it was a fair compromise. There would be a certain comfort in knowing that back up was nearby if she really did get into a jam. After all, even Watergate journalists Woodward and Bernstein had had each other.

"You'll tell him not to interfere," she insisted.

Obviously sensing her capitulation, Donelli agreed readily. "I promise. You won't even realize he's around."

"Does Oscar know you hired him?"

"No. Do you want him to know?"

"He might as well. I don't want him worrying himself to death or yanking me off this assignment."

"Then I'll tell him."

"Where are you headed now?"

"I've got a meeting with a new client, then I thought I'd check around and see what happened to Pete. I'll drop you off at your car. Bryce'll pick you up when you leave the garage. He's waiting down the block."

Minutes later he pulled into the parking garage. "Don't forget, we have dinner plans for tonight."

"Can we make it here in town?" Amanda suggested. "Now that I'm already back, I'd just as soon not drive all the way out to the country. No telling when I'll be able to wrap this up for the day, either."

"I'll meet you at your house at seven."

That was only two hours away. "I might be later."

"I'll wait."

"Without panicking?"

"That's my problem. You do your thing, just don't take any unnecessary chances."

"Promise," she agreed, brushing a kiss across his cheek.

She pulled her car out and went in search of the man police thought might have had something to do with Daria Winters's murder.

Otis Franklin's parole officer seemed almost anxious to put to rest any possible connection between his client and the murder. He agreed on the phone to produce said client for an immediate meeting at the bowling alley where they'd supposedly spent the evening on the night of the murder.

Amanda arrived first. She chatted with the guy renting shoes, with the waitress working the tables in the restaurant area, with the bartender dispensing beer. All of them agreed that Otis Franklin and his parole officer spent every Friday night bowling with two other guys. None recalled Otis missing a night.

"When you see the guy, you'll understand why I can say that with such conviction," the bartender said. "The sucker's the size of a truck."

Amanda ordered a soft drink, then carried it to a table to wait. Since it wasn't Friday, she couldn't hope to interview the suspect's usual bowling companions, but based on what she'd heard so far it would be a waste of time anyway.

She glanced at her watch. Franklin and Rodney Fisher

were late. She grew impatient, even more so than usual because she knew it was likely to be an unproductive session. Still, it wouldn't hurt to have a few quotes from these guys in her notes for the eventual article. If Otis Franklin disliked Daria Winters enough to be a suspect in her murder, there were probably others she had put away who felt the same way. It was important that Amanda capture the courtroom side of the victim.

She heard the arguing before she saw the two men. Looking in the direction of the sound, she saw the incongruous sight of a two-hundred-and-seventy-five-pound man flanked by one who was a good ten inches shorter and looked anorexic. The smaller one—Rodney Fisher, no doubt—was pale, probably because he knew Franklin could snap him in half with his bare hands if his temper got out of control.

Otis Franklin's expression was sullen, a bad omen for the interview ahead. He sat down without acknowledging Amanda's presence and snapped his fingers. The waitress materialized with a beer and a shot of whiskey. Rodney Fisher ordered a soft drink. It didn't surprise Amanda that the waitress didn't recall what was probably a standing order for the colorless man.

"Thank you for agreeing to see me," she said, pointedly addressing the comment to Franklin. He ignored her.

"Otis, answer the woman's questions," the parole officer advised.

"Ain't heard her ask one yet."

Good point, Amanda conceded. Since he clearly admired the direct approach, she went straight for the bottom line. "Did you kill Daria Winters?"

Huge brown eyes, dark with fury, regarded her intently. The meanness in those eyes was enough to make Amanda's skin crawl.

"You accusing me?"

"I'm asking you if you did it," she said evenly, keeping her gaze locked with his.

He flinched first. A flicker of something that might even have been admiration sparked in his eyes. "Hell, no, I didn't kill the broad. Me and Rodney were right here that night. Bowled two forty, two sixty-five, and two twelve. Check the sheets at the police station. We turned them in."

"Why'd you dislike her so much?"

"You ever been to prison?"

"No."

"Me, I been there two times before. It's no picnic, but I was guilty, no doubt about it. Then this bad scene goes down. Cops pick me up. This woman gets assigned to prosecute me. I was railroaded. Even a blind man could see it. She presents this pumped-up case and the next thing you know I'm behind bars again, this time for something I had no part in. You bet I hated her guts. Maybe I even threatened to get her when I got out, but I was persuaded by Rodney here to let bygones be bygones. I've cleaned up my act. Hell, I had it all cleaned up before, not that anyone noticed."

"He's telling the truth, Ms. Roberts. Otis is a changed man," the parole officer vowed as proudly as if he personally were responsible for the transformation.

She looked at him. "You probably handle a lot of people like Otis here."

"Enough."

"Any other cases where the defendants thought Daria Winters was overly aggressive?"

"All guys who get caught and land in jail think the prosecutor railroaded them, but in general Ms. Winters was fair. She had a good reputation. Accepted a plea when it was called for. Fought like a demon when she thought the defendant was guilty. In my opinion, she was even fair to Otis here, but the evidence and his past were stacked against him. His court-appointed defense lawyer was straight out of law school and wet behind the ears. He didn't object to half of the things he should have. Otis would have won on appeal, but he got out early for good behavior and it seemed pointless to continue."

Amanda absorbed the ardent defense of the parolee and shifted gears. "Do you know anything about Ms. Winters's personal life? What lawyers she hung out with? If there was anyone who was around the courthouse waiting for her after court?"

Fisher shook his head. "I'd see her in court on occasion, usually in a parole violation case, but other than that our paths didn't cross much."

Otis's brow was furrowed. Amanda turned her attention to him. "What about you?"

"Matter of fact, there was somebody. It was the first day of the trial. He was waiting for her on the courthouse steps. Next day I ran into her in the hallway outside court. I tried to joke with her about him, but she got all tense. Practically snapped my head off, said he wasn't a boyfriend, not anymore."

"But he had been in the past?" Amanda asked.

He shrugged his massive shoulders. "Guess so. They looked pretty intense."

"What did he look like?"

"Just a guy, medium build, brown hair. Expensive clothes. Handsome, if you like that all-American look. What do you call it?"

"Preppie?" Amanda supplied.

"Yeah, that was it. Preppie, like some dude who'd just graduated from Harvard and couldn't leave the house without a tie. I told her she was better off without him. Guys that uptight make me nervous."

"What did she say to that?"

"She kinda laughed then. Asked me where I'd been when she met the dude. One of the few times she seemed almost human."

Medium build, brown hair, and yuppie could probably describe at least a third of the young professional men in Atlanta, including Andrew Stone.

CHAPTER

Sixteen

AMANDA decided it was time to have another serious chat with Andrew Stone. Unfortunately it was entirely likely that the police questioning was still going on. She doubted Jim Harrison would welcome her arrival in the middle of it.

Proud of her rare discretion, she parked across from the main entrance to police headquarters and waited for the suspect to leave. Just to make sure she wasn't wasting her time, she called Harrison.

"Sorry, Ms. Roberts, the detective's in one of the interrogation rooms. I can't disturb him unless it's an emergency. Does this qualify?"

To her delight she recognized the lazy drawl of Willie Collins, the young, blond desk sergeant who'd been on the job less than a month and was still anxious to please. Prying information out of him ought to be a piece of cake.

"Is he with Andrew Stone?" she asked matter-of-factly as if such routine questions were answered automatically.

"Now you know I can't tell you something like that," he chided.

Uh-oh, she thought. She'd misjudged him. He was a stickler for rules, after all, and still too green to know when to bend them. "I could come inside and peek through the glass," she reminded him.

"That's up to you, ma'am," he said politely.

Amanda really hated being called "*ma'am*." It made her feel as if they were addressing her mother. She bit back a snappy retort. "Let's try this another way. Was Andrew Stone brought in this afternoon after his ex-wife's funeral?"

"Yes, ma'am," he said readily, probably because news of that had already been broadcast on every television and radio station in town.

"Has he left?"

"No, ma'am."

She gritted her teeth to keep from yelling at him. "Has he been charged with anything?" she asked when she could keep her tone mild.

"No, ma'am."

"Is he locked up?"

There was a faint hesitation. "No."

She grinned. Listening to all those polite *ma'ams* had been worth it. "Thanks."

"Ms. Roberts?" He sounded worried.

"Yes?"

"Did I just tell you something I wasn't supposed to?"

"I don't know," she responded innocently. "Did you?"

"Jeez, I've got to go. My other line's ringing."

"Bye-bye," she said, and settled back to wait. If Stone

didn't come out soon, there was every likelihood that he'd been charged with his ex-wife's murder. She'd give him another hour.

She dug around in her purse for a handful of jelly beans. When she found one grape and one peanut butter, she ate them together and considered it dinner. Then she picked out the pale orange mai-tai flavored ones and imagined herself on a tropical beach. With Donelli. On her honeymoon.

Donelli! Oh, hell. She glanced at her watch. She was a half hour late. She peered up and down the block for some sign of Bryce Cummings. She regretted that he had a car that seemed to blend in with every other car on the road, especially in this area where unmarked police cars of a similar model and color cruised past every minute or two. He could have radioed Joe or driven over to explain the delay. If he was nearby, though, she couldn't spot him. Which, of course, was exactly the way she'd said she wanted it.

On the off chance that Donelli might actually be in his car, she tried that number. When he didn't answer, she imagined him pacing her front porch, trying dutifully not to panic but failing miserably, stubbornly refusing to jimmy the lock so he could wait inside.

Torn between letting him continue to worry and leaving her interview with Stone for another time, and having no luck deciding between the options, she decided to call Jenny Lee and send her to the house; it was then that the car phone rang.

She grabbed it, hoping it was Donelli calling her. Instead, though, her greeting was met with absolute silence, even though the line was clearly open.

"Is anyone there?" she demanded as a faint prickle of unease crept up her neck.

"It's not too late," a raspy, unidentifiable voice finally whispered.

"Too late for what?"

"Drop the story. Let it die . . . before you do."

The phone clicked quietly.

Amanda tried to keep her hands from trembling as she replaced the car phone. Suddenly the shadows on the street seemed darker, the whisper of the wind more ominous. She tried telling herself that just because the caller had reached her on the car phone didn't mean he knew precisely where she was. The odds of her being in the car were always good. She spent a lot of time on the road. Anyone missing her at home or the office would try the car next.

One thing the incident might do, though, was prove once and for all if Andrew Stone were the prime candidate. If he was still locked away in an interrogation room with Harrison and who knew how many other witnesses, then he couldn't have made that call. She had no doubts at all that it had been made by the killer. No one else she could think of would want to warn her away from the investigation.

Leaving the car and walking that scant, unprotected distance to the police station was the hardest thing she'd ever had to do. She gripped the gun in her purse, only faintly reassured by the cold metal against her slippery palm.

Once inside, she showed her license, then checked the

gun at security and headed directly for Harrison's office. Collins, still faintly embarrassed by their earlier conversation, regarded her with a chagrined expression.

"Is he free yet?" she asked, gesturing toward Harrison's office.

"No, ma'am."

"I need to see him. It's an emergency."

He looked skeptical. "Ma'am, he said not to disturb him. I'm real sorry."

She leaned down until they were practically nose to nose and glared at him. "I think I just had a call from the killer," she said tersely. "Get Harrison for me."

He dialed at once. Less than a minute later Harrison came barreling down the hall, his tie askew, shirtsleeves rolled up, a coffee stain on the front of his shirt. The guy really was a mess. He'd never looked more wonderful. She started shaking uncontrollably the minute he came into view, her defenses suddenly relaxing.

"What the hell happened?" he demanded.

Amanda tried to keep the quiver out of her voice. She would not let him see how shaken she was. Word would get back to Donelli and Oscar, and she'd never leave the house on a decent story again.

She expelled a deep breath and spoke slowly. "I was waiting outside, hoping to catch up with Stone when you released him. My car phone rang. Some guy warned me to drop the story. Have you been with Stone for the past few minutes?" she asked.

He shook his head. "He went to the john. Let me get the officer who walked him down there, see if he had any chance to use the phone."

One of the plainclothes officers Amanda had seen at the funeral materialized in response to Harrison's call. Harrison spoke to him in an undertone, but the officer included Amanda in his response. "No, ma'am. He wasn't out of my sight and I guarantee you that he was nowhere near a phone."

Amanda's knees might have given way if she hadn't had the foresight to sit on the nearest straight-backed chair in anticipation of just such an answer. She swallowed hard. "Gentlemen, I think it's entirely possibly you're questioning the wrong man in there."

"Now, don't go jumping to conclusions, Amanda," Harrison warned. "The call could have been made by some crank and not the killer at all. We've got a lot of potential suspects out there who might have other skeletons in the closet, even if they're not responsible for the murders. You go turning over rocks, you never know what might crawl out."

The imagery was almost enough to do in her already queasy stomach.

"Who've you been talking to?" he asked.

"Today? I saw Stone at the funeral, but Hank Morton and Otis Franklin, for the most part. I'd just left Franklin."

"See. Now he's definitely the kind who wouldn't want you digging too closely into his past."

"But I doubt he'd resort to threatening phone calls. He'd probably just break my kneecaps. Don't forget, this isn't the first warning. There were those notes, one to the FBI, the other to Oscar. I guess he's finally losing patience."

His gaze narrowed. "Okay, let's think this through.

How do you suppose that warning Oscar showed us earlier got into the computer? Would someone have had to be in your office?"

"That's the most obvious answer. It's also possible that he used a modem to access the system. It's set up to take stories like that. If we're on assignment or working from home, we can just send stories from our portables to the mainframe."

"Of the suspects we have so far, who might know how to do that?"

"Stone or Morton," she said at once. "I imagine public relations types are fairly computer literate these days. Some of them work from home, then send work to the office via modem."

"Makes sense. How about Otis Franklin?"

Amanda regarded him in astonishment. "Why him? I thought he was some street punk."

Harrison grinned. "Caught you making assumptions, huh? The man robbed his employer's business by transferring funds into a dummy account. The scheme had a certain ingenious flair to it, according to his boss, who sounded like he almost regretted having to file charges. Franklin's priors were all related to computer scams of some sort."

"What about Hennessy? Does he harbor some computer skills I don't know about?"

"Doubtful, but you never know. I imagine building specifications and plans can be done on computer these days."

Amanda tried to recall Hennessy's office. It was scantily furnished. If there'd been a computer around, it hadn't been in the front office. "I think we can eliminate him, unless he's got a computer stashed at home. Karl Taylor?"

"He has a recent MBA. My guess is he had to take a few computer courses along the way."

Amanda scowled. "Well, that certainly narrows it down, doesn't it?" she said sarcastically. "How's it been going with Stone?"

"The guy was definitely obsessed with his ex-wife. He doesn't even waste time trying to hide it. Beyond that we're not able to pin him down on anything. He won't even admit to a relationship with Betsy Taylor, and we already have Karl Taylor's testimony on that. Stone concedes he knew her, but swears they were just friends." Harrison shrugged dismissively. "He could be telling the truth," he conceded. "She might have misinterpreted his intentions. The picture I got of her was someone a little shy, a little reclusive. She might have taken a show of affection and turned it into something more."

Amanda didn't buy it. "But what about other women? He had a reputation for hitting on them, despite his obsession with Lynette. I wouldn't even be surprised if he'd made a play for one of her sisters." The words were out of her mouth before she even realized she'd been thinking them.

The detective's gaze narrowed. "Why would you say that?"

"Just a funny feeling I got," she admitted. "There was a lot of hostility toward him from everyone in the family except Tricia. She didn't openly support him. She's not the kind who'd blatantly defy her parents, I don't think. But she definitely did seem sympathetic."

Harrison started to pace, his expression thoughtful.

"I recognize that look. What are you thinking?" Amanda asked.

He shook his head. "It's too bizarre."

"Try me. I love bizarre. And at the moment I'm not getting any of those little chills that tell me I'm even close to figuring out what's going on."

"We've got Stone linked to several victims," Harrison said. "We've been assuming he could have killed them, because he's the best candidate we've got. But what if this Tricia is every bit as obsessed with him as he supposedly was with his ex-wife? Maybe she's been killing off women she figures were getting in her way."

Amanda tried to envision the plain, quiet Tricia with her sweet smile going around knocking off the women in Andrew Stone's life. The theory was definitely bizarre. Downright improbable. But worth checking out, she decided.

Apparently Harrison recognized the gleam in her eyes.

"Don't you dare go marching off to visit Tricia Rogers tonight," he said adamantly. "There are too damned many dark, lonely roads between here and there."

"Who said I was going to interview her?"

"Please. Don't insult my intelligence." His expression sobered. "Amanda, you've had two warnings today alone. It's no time to take foolish chances, especially on some crazy whim."

"It was your crazy whim," she reminded him.

" 'Crazy' being the operable word. If I thought there were any chance that the theory would check out, I'd send a man down there myself."

"If you believe it's so far off base, then there's absolutely no reason for you to worry about me, now, is there?" she countered reasonably.

"I'm not worried about what will happen between you and Tricia. I'm thinking about what could happen to you between here and there if the killer happens to follow you on that dark, lonely stretch of road."

Amanda heard the worry in Harrison's voice, but she was too fascinated with the theory to wait until morning before checking it out. Of course, there was the little matter of Donelli waiting for her. She wondered how he'd feel about exchanging dinner plans for a long drive in the country. His going along for the ride ought to make just about everyone happy.

"I'll take Donelli," she promised, just to wipe that worried expression from the detective's face.

His gaze narrowed suspiciously. "That's a promise?"

"Would I lie to you?"

He shot her a rueful look. "If it suited your purposes, yes. That's what terrifies me."

CHAPTER

Seventeen

OUTSIDE police headquarters, Amanda was just about to put the key in the ignition when she caught a surreptitious movement at the side of the car. It was really no more than a shadow shifting. Nothing, she reassured herself, refusing to turn her head to look more closely. Then she heard a noise, a faint rustling sound, cloth against metal, perhaps.

Certain now that someone was trying to sneak up on her, she could feel her heart begin to thud. Adrenaline pumped through her. She opted for flight over fight, but she couldn't seem to get the damned key to slide into place because her hand was trembling so badly.

She told herself that the doors were locked, the windows closed. It gave her some vague sense of security. She tried to reinforce it by reminding herself that the killer strangled his victims. He didn't shoot them, at least not so far.

Suddenly someone rapped on the window right beside

her. She jumped as if a shot had been fired. The key fell from her grasp, as her pulse raced even faster.

She looked straight into Bryce Cummings's worried face. She'd never seen a more welcome sight.

"You okay, Amanda?" he asked loudly enough to be heard through the still closed window.

She closed her eyes as a sigh of relief whispered through her. She rolled down the window. "Just fine."

"I saw you take off and go inside earlier. You looked jumpy, but Joe told me to steer clear unless it looked like something was going down."

"It was nothing. Actually, I looked for you. Joe said you'd be around. I didn't see the car."

"I was around the corner where I could keep an eye on you without being seen by anyone else. Not to worry. I could have gotten here if you'd needed me. You heading home now?"

"Yeah. I'm going by the house to meet Joe. There's no need for you to come along. He'll be there." She paused. "On second thought, maybe I could use you as a buffer. He'll probably be furious because I'm late."

"No, he's cool. I've been checking in with him. I'll follow along, just the same. Make sure you get there okay."

Amanda saw little point in arguing with him. Donelli was paying him to keep watch, and she'd agreed to let him. He was just being dutiful. She should be grateful. She managed a smile that was almost sincere. "Thanks, Bryce."

At home, she found Donelli sitting patiently on the porch, a stack of unopened mail on the table beside him.

He waved to Bryce, who tooted his horn as he continued on past.

"You taking over his duties now?" she asked.

"Yeah, I'm cheaper and a whole lot more dedicated. Any objections?"

"That depends."

"On?"

"On whether you're in the mood to grab some take-out Chinese and drive down to see Lynette Rogers's family."

"What on earth for?"

"Jim Harrison mentioned an off-the-wall theory earlier. I think it's worth checking out."

"And you have to do this tonight?"

"By tomorrow he'll have done it himself."

"And you absolutely have to be there first, ahead of the police? Hasn't it occurred to you that if Harrison thought it really was a viable theory, he'd be on the road himself?"

"True."

"Is he?"

"No," she admitted.

"Well then . . ."

"I'd still like to go." She leaned down and kissed him. "We could talk about wedding plans in the car."

He raised one quizzical brow. "Is that a bribe?"

"It is if it's working."

He sighed heavily. "Let me toss this mail inside and then we'll go."

As it turned out, the discussion of wedding plans had to be temporarily shelved. Thirty miles outside of Atlanta someone with very accurate aim shot out both of Donelli's rear tires. The timing was damned near perfect for anyone hoping to cause a fatal accident. The blasts sent the car spinning off the road and straight toward a towering old oak that already had a marker on it from the last fatality on that particular curve of highway. Amanda could read the engraved lettering on the plaque as they careened toward the tree: **IN MEMORY OF . . .**

The rest was lost when, at the last second, Donelli wrenched the steering wheel to the right. The tree crumpled the front bumper on the driver's side with a sickening crunch. As the car skidded to a stop, they were both thrown forward, then jerked back into place by their seat belts.

When Amanda could breathe again, she glanced over. "You okay?"

Donelli looked more exasperated than injured. "Has it occurred to you that after owning the same car in New York for ten years, I seem to be having a real run of bad luck with them down here?"

She smiled weakly. "Maybe it has something to do with the company you keep."

Nothing dissuaded Amanda from going out to see Tricia Rogers—not even dealing with the Highway Patrol, a team of solicitous paramedics, and the inconvenience of having to go all the way back to Atlanta in a tow truck to get her own car. If anything, it only firmed her resolve to get to the bottom of the killings as quickly as possible.

"It'll be midnight when we get there," Donelli protested.

"Then she'll be half-asleep. All the better to get the truth out of her."

"We stay at my place afterward," he bargained.

"Okay," she agreed, recognizing a final offer when she heard one.

This time the trip was uneventful. Tricia Rogers was, in fact, asleep when they arrived. So was everyone else in the household. No one appreciated being awakened by a reporter and a private investigator.

Once awakened, however, they were not inclined to leave Tricia alone in the living room with company, especially company intent on asking probing questions. Dressed in robes, they trailed into the kitchen, where Mrs. Rogers put on a pot of coffee—the real stuff, not decaf.

Mrs. Rogers studied Amanda as if she were the first media person she'd ever seen up close, an alien being in this quiet part of the state. "I'm sorry I wasn't up to talking to you the other day," she said. "It's been a difficult time for all of us."

"I'm sure it has been," Amanda said sympathetically. "And I really am sorry to bother you and your family so late, but I wanted to ask a few more questions about Andrew."

"The police are holding him, aren't they?" Tricia said worriedly. She was stirring her coffee nervously, even though she'd added neither sugar nor cream.

"Right now they're just interrogating him," Amanda reassured her. "He hasn't been charged with anything."

"Well, I can't imagine why he hasn't been," Jessica commented with an indignant sniff. "There's not a doubt in my mind he killed Lynette."

Mr. Rogers pounded the table with his fist. "That's enough of that. I may not be real fond of the man, but a man's innocent 'til proven guilty. That's the way our system works."

"I know what I know," Jessica insisted, her stubborn gaze clashing with her father's."

"What do you think you know?" Amanda asked.

"Just that he always was a crazy man when it came to Lynette. He would have been jealous of a cat if she showed it any affection."

As Jessica answered, Amanda kept her gaze pinned on Tricia, saw the swift rise in color in her cheeks.

"Tricia," she said gently, "what do you think? Do you think Andrew's guilty?"

Tricia glanced around worriedly, as if afraid of offending anyone, then shook her head defiantly. "No. No, I don't."

"Why?"

"You don't understand him," she said, shooting an accusing glance at the other members of the family. "None of you. He has these powerful emotions that build up inside him. If Lyn had loved him the way a wife should love her husband, everything would have been just fine."

Amanda wondered if that depth of loyalty was the kind that could turn deadly. "Were you and Andrew close?"

Mr. Rogers's mouth dropped open. "Now just what are you implying about my daughter?"

Amanda met his indignant gaze without wavering. "I'm just asking if there was a special bond of some kind between Tricia and Andrew."

Tricia was already nodding, oblivious of her father's distress at the faintly suggestive nature of the question.

"We could talk," she said. "He understood me. Better than anyone," she added with another touch of defiance.

Amanda exchanged a look with Donelli, then turned back to Tricia. "Did you ever know a woman named Betsy Taylor?"

Tricia hesitated a long time before answering. Because she was trying to recall? Amanda wondered. Or because she needed to cover her tracks?

"The name sounds familiar," she said eventually. "But I don't believe I know her."

"Lauren Blakely?"

She shook her head immediately. "No."

"Joyce Landers?"

Mr. Rogers rose then, cutting off whatever Tricia's answer might have been. "I think that's about enough," he said quietly. "You've intruded on us long enough."

Apparently no one other than Lynette's father realized the direction in which Amanda's questions were leading. They seemed startled by the rudeness of his dismissal.

"Now, Father," Mrs. Rogers said, then was silenced by his fierce scowl.

Amanda could tell there was no point in lingering. "Thank you for answering my questions," she said to Tricia. "If you'd like to talk about Andrew again, give me a call."

She slid one of her cards into Tricia's hand despite the disapproval she could read in Mr. Rogers's eyes.

"She'll have nothing more to say," he said.

After they were outside, Amanda looked at Donelli. "What'd you think?"

"I think that she had a terrible crush on her older sister's husband, but I don't think that meant she went on a jealous rampage and killed every other woman with whom he came into contact."

"Stranger things have happened."

"You saw her, Amanda. She doesn't look the least bit athletic, much less mean. Do you honestly think she's capable of strangling anyone with her bare hands or slicing her sister with a knife in the process?"

Amanda sighed. "No," she admitted reluctantly. "Not really. To top it off, she's totally blind to the possibility that Andrew might be guilty of the killings. Given the fact that she seems to be otherwise reasonably intelligent, that lends some credence to my hunch that Andrew had nothing to do with the murders."

"When did you jump to that conclusion?" Donelli inquired, clearly amused by this latest gut impression that seemed to fly in the face of the evidence.

Whoops! She forced a weak smile. "When I had a call in the car from the killer and I discovered there was no way Andrew could have made it."

All traces of amusement fled, turning his expression darkly forbidding. "And when was that?"

She saw no point in hiding the rest. "Earlier tonight, when I was staking out police headquarters waiting for him to be released."

Donelli started to speak but cut off the exasperated response in midsentence. "Forget it. You were just doing you job."

"Yes, I was," she said quietly, grateful for the concession. "I guess this trip was a waste of time after all, though."

Donelli grinned at her. "Not entirely. You get to spend the night with me."

As compensations went, Amanda figured this one wasn't bad at all.

When Amanda dragged herself out of bed the next morning, the sun was already high in the sky and Donelli was nowhere in sight. A note on the kitchen counter beside a fresh pot of coffee said he was putting in his tomato plants.

She poured herself a cup of coffee and wandered out barefoot to hunt for him. The grass was still cool and covered with dew in the shade, but when she reached the field where he was working, the freshly turned earth was warm and dry beneath her feet. Under pain of torture, she might even concede it felt good. It took her back to childhood summer days, running barefoot over the grounds at her grandmother's house on Long Island.

"You let me oversleep," she said, leaning down to brush a kiss across his bare shoulder. The skin had been warmed by the sun.

"You needed it. I called Oscar and told him you were running late."

"Thanks." She drew in a deep breath of the fresh morning air.

He observed her with a smile. "Nothing quite like that smell, huh?"

"I guess not."

"You ready to set the date for making this your permanent place of residence?" The question was asked casually, while he continued tucking tiny seedlings into the soil.

Amanda bit back an easy "Yes" and asked the question that had been troubling her more and more recently. "What about kids, Joe? That's something we never talked about."

He glanced up at her, clearly surprised. "How do you feel about it?"

"What would we do on a night like last night?"

"There are baby-sitters and housekeepers. People manage."

She sighed with regret. She'd been hoping irrationally that maybe it wouldn't be an issue. "So, you do want children? I thought so. I saw how you were with Pete the other night."

"And how was that?"

"Natural. You listened to him. You really cared about him. You'd make a wonderful father."

He chuckled. "So, ergo, I must have kids of my own? If that were true, we wouldn't be having this conversation, Amanda. You listened. You cared every bit as much as I did. And I'm getting the feeling here that you're not so sure about wanting children of your own."

"No, I'm not," she said, relieved to have the admission out in the open.

"Is this something we have to decide before we get married, especially since it's clear that neither of us has really strong feelings pro or con? Couldn't we just work it out?"

She studied him closely. "That depends. You really wouldn't mind not having children?"

"Every cop, unless he's totally blind and self-absorbed, knows that parenting is difficult. I saw a lot of my friends wind up divorced, trying to be a father from a distance. It always seemed to me that some people in certain professions just aren't meant to have families."

She heard the wistful note in his voice, even if he didn't. "You're not a cop anymore," she reminded him, hunkering down beside him so she could look straight into his eyes.

"No. But I seem to be in love with a woman who courts danger just the way I used to."

"If I said yes, though, if I said I wanted children, maybe not now, but someday, you'd want them, too, wouldn't you? Tell the truth."

His gaze came up and met hers. "Yes, I suppose I would," he said cautiously.

Amanda tried to balance her fears with the realities, saying aloud what she'd known inside all along. "You're the strong one, the steady one. A kid would be lucky to have you at home after school, even if he or she had a mom who was off chasing bad guys, right?"

There was no mistaking the flare of hope in his eyes. "We could make it work, Amanda. If the time ever came . . ."

She reached for his hand and rubbed her thumb across the scarred knuckles. So much warmth. So much strength. A kid would be lucky. *She* would be lucky.

"How would you feel about a week from Saturday?" she said softly. "If this story's wrapped up."

He grinned. "It'll be wrapped up," he vowed, "if I have to catch this damned killer myself."

CHAPTER

Eighteen

ALL the way into town, Amanda thought about her commitment to marry Donelli and about their conversation about children. She also thought about the boy who spawned it, Pete Jackson. Why hadn't he shown up at Donelli's the day before? Was there more trouble for him at home? Had he run away again? And if he had, why hadn't he turned to her or to Joe, when he'd obviously come to trust them?

When she reached the *Inside Atlanta* office, it was deserted. Atlanta's downtown office buildings were almost eerie on Sundays, with the silent corridors and darkened hallways. She felt a vague uneasiness until the office lights were bright overhead and she was at her desk. She promptly reached for a phone book and looked for the number for Pete Jackson's father. Surprisingly, it was listed. On an impulse, she dialed.

An older woman answered, her voice scratchy. "Jackson residence." She managed to cut three syllables into two by leaving out the *i*, res-dence.

"Is Pete there?"

"Who?"

"Pete Jackson."

"Nobody here by that name. You sure you have the right place?"

"Do the Jacksons have a son, about eleven years old?"

"No, ma'am. Two girls, Melissa and Laura Lee. They're all at church now."

"Thank you," Amanda said, and slowly hung up.

How odd. Maybe the woman had been confused. She'd sounded old. Perhaps she was only visiting the house or was new to the family. Perhaps she'd been instructed to lie, on the off chance that authorities were checking into the troublesome Pete.

But to flat-out deny his existence?

Intrigued despite her need to get on with the task of checking out leads in the murders, she went to the photo files. *Inside Atlanta*'s collection of photos wasn't terribly extensive, because it was a relatively new magazine. But politicians running for office in the last election had deluged the place with campaign photos. Surely there would be one of Pete Jackson's father.

She found the file at once. There were two photos in it, one of the senior Jackson taken during the previous spring's Dogwood Festival. An attractive man in his late thirties, he gazed at the camera with sincere blue eyes and a practiced politician's easy smile, while he clasped the hand of one of the festival's organizers. The incredible flowering dogwood displayed their finest blossoms around them. April in Georgia was hard to beat for sheer beauty.

The second photo was the one Amanda had been hoping to find. A professional family portrait, done in black and white, it showed Jackson and his wife. She was wearing one of those floaty chiffon numbers Bryce had described. She looked demure and utterly feminine, except for that avaricious glint of steel in her eyes. With them were two perfect children, dressed in their Sunday best.

Both girls.

So, Pete had lied. More incredibly, so had Bryce Cummings. Why? To protect Pete's real identity?

Thoroughly baffled, Amanda thought back over the conversation that night in the park. Pete had planted the idea of his identity without ever mentioning a last name. Had he done it deliberately to mislead them? If so, why pick a public figure? So that she and Joe would jump to an obvious conclusion, given his resemblance to Councilman Jackson? It had worked, hadn't it? But what if they had known that Jackson had no sons? Had Bryce and the kid left themselves an out?

She tried to recall what exactly Bryce had said. Had he actually confirmed their assumption or merely gone along to protect a confidential client? She couldn't recall his precise words clearly enough to know for sure.

At any rate, Joe was going to be distraught to discover that they had no way of learning Pete's real identity. He'd worry himself sick over that poor kid, unless Bryce decided to clear up the mystery.

At a dead end with that, she reluctantly turned her attention back to the murders. She couldn't shake the feeling that there was something obvious she was missing.

She went back through her notes page by page, line by

line. It was a tedious process, one that might have driven her crazy if it had taken all afternoon. Fortunately she discovered what had been nagging at her when she came to one of her earliest conversations with Jim Harrison.

He'd said that they'd linked Lynette Rogers and Lauren Blakely to the psychologist Joyce Landers through canceled checks. What if there were other canceled checks, including one that Marnie Evans had written to whomever she'd had that business meeting with on the afternoon she'd died? It might even have come in a month or two after the police had gone through her original bank statements.

She called Harrison. He didn't fail her. Sunday or not, he was at his desk. He sounded too tense and weary to waste time on pleasantries. She got straight to the point.

"I need to go through some of the evidence," she told him. "Can you arrange it?"

"What are you looking for?"

"Canceled checks, starting with whatever you have for Marnie Evans."

"Why her?"

"Because she had an appointment that afternoon we've never been able to track down. I wondered if she might not have paid someone that day. If it was the killer, maybe he waited to cash the check. Or maybe there's a notation in her checkbook."

When he didn't offer any argument, Amanda knew she'd triggered his imagination.

"I'll pull what we've got," he said. "How soon can you get here?"

"I'm on my way. I'll be there in fifteen minutes."

When she arrived at the police station, Amanda found Jim Harrison seated behind a desk stacked with little piles of canceled checks, topped off by checkbooks ranging from fancy to standard bank issue.

"Anything?"

"I thought I'd wait for you."

She grinned. "Sometimes you are such a gentleman. Which one is Marnie's?"

He pointed to the gray leather checkbook with its standard gray blank checks, these from Peach State Savings and Loan. Amanda flipped through the dated entries in front until she found the day of the murder.

One check for fourteen fifty-seven had been written for dry cleaning. The next notation, to a franchise haircutting salon, was for twenty-five. She'd spent thirty-four dollars and sixteen cents at the grocery store. The last check, for four hundred dollars, was made out to cash.

"Nothing," she said, filled with disappointment. "She picked up her dry cleaning. she got her hair done, stopped by the grocery store, then got cash from the bank. That's it."

Jim Harrison nodded, his expression thoughtful. "Maybe it's not nothing." Carefully he picked through the checks until he found the one made out to cash. Handling it gingerly by one corner, he lifted it out and then dropped it into a plastic evidence bag.

"Why?" Amanda said. Slowly she answered the question for herself. "You think that check for cash might still have been for the person she met with, right?"

"Exactly. How many people do you know who go to

the bank *after* they've run all their errands? Wouldn't she be more likely to pick up cash first?"

"Depends on the route she needed to take," Amanda countered. "Could be that's the order things were in between the office and home, but I see your point."

"Okay, say you're right. Let's check it out."

He pulled out a phone book and looked up the addresses. Amanda checked them against the huge street map on his office wall.

First Marnie Evans's family practice clinic, then the dry cleaners, then the hairdresser, then the grocery, then the bank. The line Amanda sketched with her pencil went in logical order until she tried to connect it with the bank. Then she had to back track to a branch two blocks on the other side of the clinic.

"Bingo," she said softly. "And that check could have the killer's fingerprints."

He shrugged. "His and probably dozens of others by this time, but we'll never know until we try."

"Let's go through these others," Amanda said with renewed enthusiasm.

She found the stack for Lauren Blakely, glanced through the checkbook, going straight to the last entry: six hundred dollars, cash.

The final entry in Joyce Landers's checkbook was five hundred and fifty dollars, cash.

Amanda's adrenaline began to pump, this time with the excitement that always came with a breakthrough in a major story. She could see from Jim Harrison's cautiously optimistic expression that he felt exactly the same way.

Daria Winters was next. Four hundred, cash.

Betsy Taylor, two hundred, cash.

By the time Amanda picked up Lynette Rogers's checkbook, her fingers were trembling. Seven hundred, cash.

"This is it," she said, slowly meeting Jim Harrison's gaze. "These women were all paying big bucks to someone with checks made out to cash on the day they died. That has to be the answer."

"But who?" he said, his voice measured. Even so it betrayed his excitement. "A blackmailer?"

Amanda tried to make that fit with what she knew about each of the victims. It didn't make sense with anyone except possibly Joyce Landers. Even in her case, Amanda had found no real evidence to substantiate the rumors that she was a lesbian. Jenny Lee had questioned dozens of acquaintances, and all had agreed that Joyce maintained a very private personal life but was definitely heterosexual.

The others had all seemed to lead exemplary lives. Only their relationships with men in some instances had been rocky. Had they gotten hooked up with some guy who was into kinky sex? Some guy who'd taken compromising pictures? It just didn't ring true.

Karl Taylor, of course, had been desperate enough for drug money to resort to blackmailing. But what could he possibly have gotten on all those women?

Maybe she'd missed something, though. "Have you found any evidence that any of them had anything in their lives over which they could be blackmailed?" she asked the detective.

He shook his head. "No."

"Me either."

"Maybe we should go through these checkbooks again, see if there's a pattern to these cash disbursements."

He took three. Amanda took the others. She found plenty of checks written to cash, but when she began to study the dates, she realized that in each case there were two or three, sometimes four, written for amounts similar to the final entry and always on the same day of the week as the murder.

When he'd finished, Harrison confirmed a similar pattern.

"That fits a blackmail pattern all right," Amanda said. "Or a regular appointment of some kind."

"The patterns only go back a month or two at most, though," he said. "There are cash checks before that, but the day of the week they were written and the amounts vary just the way you'd expect. Did they finally take a stand and cut off the blackmailer? Then get killed by him?"

It was as good a scenario as any, but without any evidence they couldn't link it to any of the suspects. So far.

Even though she was disappointed that they couldn't immediately identify the killer, Amanda still recognized the significance of what they had discovered. Now all she needed to do was go through her notes one more time and then patiently sift through the facts until the relevant ones became clearer. She was convinced she finally had all of the pieces. If only she could make them fit together, she'd know who had committed the murders and why.

What she needed, in fact, was a quiet evening at home, by herself. No interruptions. No group speculation.

"Let's take some time to think about it," she suggested. "If I come up with anything, I'll give you a call."

"In the meantime, I'll pull these checks and have them examined for prints. Maybe we'll get lucky and find some matches among them."

"Maybe we'll get even luckier and find one that's on file."

Jim Harrison nodded wearily, clearly a man ready for a break in the case and willing to grasp at straws. "Yeah," he said. "I figure the odds on that are only one in maybe eighty, ninety million."

Amanda patted his hand. "Whatever the odds, they're better than what we had just a couple of hours ago. Remember that."

The reminder seemed to bolster his flagging energy. He was already pulling out a stack of evidence bags and picking through checks by the time she closed the door to his office.

C H A P T E R

Nineteen

AMANDA fixed herself a cup of tea, a peanut-butter-and-jelly sandwich, and went out on her deck to think. A full moon bathed the backyard in silvery light. From down the street she could hear a neighbor's dog barking, then a responding yowl from farther away.

She sipped her tea and took a bite of her sandwich, then left both sitting untouched on the table beside her.

She was still missing something. She had a feeling it had to do with the fact that all six women were financially secure, capable of paying out large sums of money for something they didn't want anyone else to know about. Otherwise, why not make the checks out directly to whatever company or individual they were dealing with?

It could have been blackmail, but maybe there were other possible explanations.

Obviously it had something to do with privacy, but what? What would she pay big bucks for, but hide? Therapy, maybe, but the women who were in treatment with

Joyce Landers hadn't bothered to hide that. Those checks were clearly recorded.

Were they lonely? Had each been taken in by some gigolo, maybe after responding to some personal ad? Possibly. But the men in their lives, for the most part, were known. There was no indication any of the women had been involved in a secret relationship, one they'd paid to keep hidden from the world out of fear or shame.

Frustrated with her inability to put it together, she finally wandered inside. She paced through the house, trying to keep her head clear so that any brainstorms would have room to move in. Unfortunately brainstorms seemed to be in short supply.

Maybe if she stopped thinking about it altogether . . . She sat down at her desk. She'd catch up on some of her own bills. Perhaps writing out all those checks would make her feel a connection to the other women. She rolled her eyes at the idiocy of that idea.

An unopened stack of mail sat atop the magazines that had arrived a few days earlier. She reached for the first one, then noticed that it was addressed to Donelli. She remembered that he had brought in his mail the previous night and dumped it on the desk before they'd taken off to see Tricia Rogers. Obviously he hadn't given it another thought.

She sorted through the envelopes to see if anything looked important. A couple of flyers made out to "Resident," a bill from the phone company, one plain envelope with no return address. The last one triggered her curiosity. She called his house.

"You okay?" he asked at once. "How'd it go on the story today?"

"Lousy. I thought we had something, but I can't make it fit," she said, taking the last question first. "But I'm home. I'm safe. I just discovered your mail sitting here on the desk. Who's writing you letters with no return address on the outside? You hiding something from me?"

"As if I'd dare. You'd have it figured out by noon the same day you got suspicious. Anyway, it's probably from my latest client. Discretion is very important to her. She even makes her checks out to cash rather than to me."

Amanda let the offhand remark sink in. "Oh, my God," she said quietly. "That's it."

"What's it? What are you talking about?"

"The link," she said excitedly. "Don't you see? I'll bet every one of the victims had hired a private detective."

"That's one helluva leap. Why on earth would you think that?"

She explained about the checks made out to cash. "And every one of those women was involved in a relationship that had turned sour or had something else going on in their lives that might have caused them to hire a private eye. I'd forgotten that it's getting more and more common for women to do that, especially if they get bad vibes from some man or are worried about AIDS or something. They might want to know if he's cheating or if he has something in his past he's hiding from them."

Donelli was astonishingly quiet.

"Well, say something," she said.

"It makes sense," he admitted. "The woman I'm working for does fit the profile of the victims. She's worried that the man she's sleeping with isn't being honest about other sexual partners and she's terrified of AIDS."

"As well she should be. Why's she sleeping with him, if she has doubts?"

"I guess she didn't start to have them until the last couple of months."

"Donelli, is Bryce supposed to be around here tonight? Maybe I should ask him, too. I'll bet he's had similar clients. If we can find out if they all hired the same detective, maybe he saw something. He might be able to give us some idea what was going on in the lives of these women."

"Bryce should be keeping an eye on the house. I'll beep him, tell him to stop in. He probably knows more about local PIs than I do."

"In the meantime, I'll call Harrison and tell him what we're thinking. Legitimate PIs have their prints on file, don't they?"

"They should."

"Then if there are prints on those checks, a match should be in the computer. I'll call you back as soon as we find out anything."

She disconnected Donelli, then immediately dialed Jim Harrison's office. When she'd alerted him, she remembered that she'd never spoken with Kelsey Hall. Maybe she and Lynette had been close enough that she would know whether Lynette had ever hired a private detective to keep an eye or Andrew Stone or for any other reason, for that matter.

As soon as she had the stockbroker on the line, she got straight to the point. "Is it possible that she was paying a

PI to keep an eye on her ex-husband so she'd know when he was back in town?"

"She didn't need a private eye for that. Andy called her half a dozen times a day at least. She always knew exactly where he was."

"Oh," Amanda said, her voice flat.

"Did you know that she was considering a reconciliation, though?"

"With Andy Stone?"

"Yep. I think he'd just worn her down, but she still didn't quite trust him. It's entirely possible that she might have hired someone to prove whether he was telling the truth about the other women in his life. He'd sworn to her that his affairs were all over. If you ask me, that was impossible for someone like Andy. The man would flirt with a bus if it stayed in place long enough."

Kelsey Hall didn't make the observation affectionately. "I still can't figure out what she saw in him," she added. "Maybe on a bad day all that obsessiveness seemed like love. It just gave me the chills."

Amanda didn't want to get sidetracked into a discussion of Andy Stone's personality flaws or Kelsey Hall's reaction to them. "But you don't know for a fact that she'd hired a PI?"

"No, I'm sorry. If she did, though, she probably would have gotten the name through one of our security guys. John Morgan, the head of security, used to hang out with Lynette sometimes. You could check with him tomorrow."

"Thanks, Kelsey. You've been a big help."

Amanda hung up and considered who might know if one of the other victims might have hired a private eye.

Maybe William Hennessy. He'd had a troubled marriage. Had it been because he'd been cheating on his wife? Had she hired someone to prove it? Wouldn't he know if she had?

She called the house. His wife sounded young and suspicious when Amanda identified herself. Because she, too, didn't trust her husband?

"He's at the office," she said grudgingly.

"Thanks. I'll try him there. By the way, congratulations. he told me when I interviewed him that you're expecting a baby," Amanda said, just to relieve the poor woman's mind about her own intentions where William Hennessy was concerned.

"Thanks. We're really excited about it," the woman responded in a voice suddenly free of tension. "If you don't catch William at the office, do you want me to have him call you?"

"I'd appreciate it," Amanda said, though she had every intention of tracking him down long before he had a chance to get home again.

She caught him less than a minute later, still at the office, still sounding despondent when he realized it was not a prospective client on the line. With a baby on the way, could he have been desperate enough to try blackmailing his ex-wife? Amanda dismissed the idea almost as soon as it had formed. Stick to the obvious.

"I'll get right to the point," she told him. "Was Lauren ever suspicious that you might be having an affair?"

"What the hell kind of question is that?"

Amanda lost patience. "Look, I don't give a damn about your marital infidelities, but it's entirely possible that Lauren did. If so, would she have hired a private investigator to follow you, to get her proof?"

He exhaled slowly. "Okay, I did have an affair while we were married. It was a mistake and it didn't last long. It's certainly plausible that she might have gotten suspicious and hired a detective, but she never admitted it to me, and I certainly never caught one lurking in the bushes. What difference does it make?"

"Because I'm beginning to think that all of these women were either being blackmailed or had hired a detective they were paying in cash. It's just a theory, but if I can prove it with one victim, the rest may fall into place. I figure the detective might have seen something that could help the investigation."

"I wish I could help you, but I just don't know." he said wearily. "I'm sorry."

Damn, damn, damn! She wasn't getting anywhere with this. Maybe Jim Harrison was having better luck. She started to dial his office. She'd hit the fourth number when she heard the line go dead.

With chilling certainty, she recognized at once what was happening. Pieces that only an instant before had been disgustingly elusive suddenly tumbled into place so rapidly that it left her head spinning.

This was no power outage. No one had accidentally clipped a cable. The killer had been tapping her phone, had heard everything she and Donelli had speculated about. Had heard her conversations with Kelsey Hall and William Hennessy and knew that she was only days, maybe hours, away from identifying him.

With the silencing of her phone, cutting her off from

help, Amanda knew with gut-wrenching certainty that the timetable had just been cut to minutes, maybe seconds.

That's how long it was likely to be before he came through a door or a window, confirming what she'd already begun to suspect the instant the phone line went dead, what she should have guessed the minute she'd realized that Pete wasn't who he'd claimed to be, but someone probably paid to manipulate that supposedly chance meeting in Piedmont Park.

The killer was Bryce Cummings, ironically the very man Donelli had hired to protect her.

CHAPTER

Twenty

THE muted sound of careful footsteps sounded on the deck. With Bryce closing in on the back door, flight seemed the obvious solution, but there was no time. Amanda knew she'd never get all the way out of the house, much less to her car phone, before he could get to her.

She could create a commotion, run screaming to a neighbor's, throw a heavy object through a window. Self-defense classes were very specific about those options. But she figured by the time anyone reacted, she could be dead. Besides, she told herself, if she just kept her wits about her, she could handle this . . . and get her story.

She glanced frantically around the kitchen until she spotted her purse. Keeping her gaze locked on the back-door knob, which was rattling now, she inched over to the kitchen counter where she'd tossed it earlier. She reached inside, closed her hand around the gun, and released it slowly. She wanted to know it was there, just in case.

She switched on the tape recorder, left it inside her

purse as well, then draped the shoulder strap over the back of a chair. She'd damn well have proof when this nightmare ended. Seated, she should be able to reach the gun without much effort. She sat back down at the kitchen table and tested her theory just as the latch on the back door finally popped.

She glanced up from her notes as if she were merely surprised rather than terrified. Knowing she could get to that gun kept her more confident than she had any right to be.

"Bryce? What's going on?" She was proud of the fact that her voice didn't quiver at all. Maybe her nonchalance would calm him.

Hell, maybe she was completely wrong about this.

He matched her cool facade with one of his own. "I thought I heard some noise from in here. I thought I'd better come and check on you. Everything okay?"

She smiled. "I'm just fine. The phone went dead a minute ago, though."

He continued with the charade of solicitous protector. He walked over, picked it up, and listened. "You're right. Someone must have cut a cable someplace. I'll go put in a call to the phone company in a minute, as soon as I check around a little."

"Do you think it's the phone, or could someone have cut the line to the house?" she responded, watching his face for some sign of emotion. Nothing. He was absolutely cool and, therefore, doubly dangerous. "By the way, I'm glad you came in. I wanted to talk to you anyway."

This time his gaze did narrow just a little. "Oh?"

"Sit down. You want some coffee or a beer?"

"No thanks."

He didn't sit, either. He leaned against the counter, the stance intentionally casual, but it couldn't cover the sudden, coiled tension. Amanda's gaze drifted to his hands. Large and powerful, he had them clenched at his sides. Thinking of those six strangled women, she shuddered and looked away.

"How long have you been a private detective now?"

"Four or five years."

"What kinds of cases?"

"The usual. Skip traces for creditors. Nasty divorces. Occasional work for some lawyers I used to deal with when I was on the force."

"Do you ever get hired by women?"

"About as often as men. That's a weird question," he said, looking more agitated than he had at any point up until now. He was cracking his knuckles in what seemed to be an unconscious nervous habit.

"I just wondered. It seems to me that more and more women might be hiring detectives to check out men they don't trust, husbands, boyfriends, maybe. You know how things are these days with relationships."

"Yeah, I do."

"I'm wondering if there isn't a story in that, modern romance, scary times, that sort of thing."

He didn't seem nearly as enthralled with the concept as she was. In fact, he seemed to be staring off at something she couldn't see. Amanda warned herself to keep him off balance, to switch directions so he wouldn't guess exactly what she was going after. Maybe he wouldn't realize that she'd put most of it together by now.

"Are you married, Bryce?"

His wary gaze shot back at her. "Me? Why?"

"Just wondered. A PI's schedule must be tough on a marriage."

"No. I got divorced a couple of years back. Being a cop is hell on a marriage, too."

Amanda considered the timing. The divorce had come not when he was still on the force, but only a short time before the first murder. Had he been so embittered by losing his wife that he'd started taking it out on other women?

"What happened? Too many long hours?"

"The hours, the danger. She figured I was getting it on with every chick who got turned on by a uniform. Actually hired a guy to tail me," he said, his face turning an angry shade of red. "Bitch."

So that was the motivation, Amanda thought. He blamed his ex-wife for catching him in the act of cheating on her. He probably hadn't been able to bring himself to take out his fury on her, so he'd gone after other women doing the same thing. It was too soon, though, to try to wring a confession from him. She wanted him off kilter again.

"How's Pete doing?"

He regarded her blankly. "Who?"

"The runaway you were chasing the night we met."

"Oh, yeah. Pete." He shrugged. "Haven't heard."

"Funny thing. I happened to look in the Jackson file the

other day and saw a photo of his family. He doesn't have a son."

For a moment Bryce seemed totally thrown. "Jackson?" he said hurriedly. "Who said his name was Jackson? It's Wallace. Pete Wallace."

Amanda let it go. "Oh. My mistake." She wanted desperately to pour herself another cup of coffee—or a good stiff drink—but she wasn't about to move from the table and its reassuring proximity to her gun.

"Did you ever work a case tailing a guy named William Hennessy?" she asked, deciding to mention the men in the case rather than the victims.

His gaze was instantly watchful. "Hennessy? Nah. I don't think so. Even if I had, you know I couldn't talk about it."

"How about Karl Taylor? His cousin thought he'd started using cocaine again. I'm guessing she tried to prove it."

He began to pace. "I told you, I can't talk about cases. You've been around Donelli enough. You should know that."

She smiled. "Never hurts to ask." She hesitated, trying to decide if she should go for broke. Not quite yet. "How'd you happen to know Martin Luther Washington was back in town?"

He stopped pacing, his expression faintly puzzled. It was a good act.

"Who?" he asked.

"The guy police think might have been involved in Marnie Evans's murder. Jim Harrison mentioned you'd alerted them that he was back."

"The family hired me to keep a look out for him."

"How'd they happen to pick you? Did you know Marnie?"

"We'd met. I play basketball occasionally with some of the guys who work with her, the other doctors. Hank Morton's in that crowd, too."

She nodded. "That's right. I saw you together at Lynette's funeral. I assumed you were there because Joe'd asked you to keep an eye on me."

"I was, but I'd have been there anyway."

"Because of Hank?"

His pacing resumed, and he left the question unanswered.

"Or were you there because of Andy Stone? Did you know him well?"

"Indirectly," he admitted, regarding her with amazingly guileless eyes.

He came up behind her, rested his hands on the back of her chair. Amanda was chillingly aware that those hands were scant inches from her neck. She shoved the chair back and stood, then faced him apologetically.

"Sorry. I just thought I ought to start dinner. I'm expecting Joe soon."

"Oh?" he said, his amusement obvious.

Knowing that nothing at all had been said about dinner on the phone, Amanda prayed she could convince him that the plans had been made earlier. She glanced at the kitchen clock. It was nearly seven now. "When I left his place this morning, we figured we'd get together for dinner about seven, seven-thirty."

It was a risk. Either he would back off or he would decide he had only minutes left in which to kill her. Judging from the menacing look in his eyes, he'd decided to make his move now.

He stepped close enough that she could smell the spearmint scent of the gum she'd seen him chewing from time to time.

"You're quite a woman," he said softly. "It's too bad you're so damned nosy. Like all those others, you just couldn't leave well enough alone. How the hell's a guy supposed to get a break in life, if some woman's always on his case?"

Fighting the bile rising in her throat, she kept her gaze steady and tried to put the chair—and the gun—between her and him. "I don't know what you mean."

His smile was no longer quite so pleasant. "Oh, I'm sure you do."

He reached for her and kicked the chair aside in the same instant, the action so quick and so well timed that Amanda was caught completely off guard. His fingers dug into her shoulders. To her horror he dragged her close, then ground his mouth against hers in a mockery of a kiss.

Just then the back door crashed open and a boy's voice, filled with righteous indignation, screamed an agonized, "No!"

Both Amanda and Bryce whirled to see Pete—or whoever he was—standing there, his expression furious, a long barbecue fork clenched in his fist. Even as they faced him in stunned silence, he ran toward Bryce with that fork, taking deadly aim at his midsection.

Bryce knocked it aside, then slammed his own far more powerful fist into Pete's face. Blood spurted from his nose and mouth, but the kid was a fighter. He barreled into Bryce's stomach headfirst.

Even as Bryce's hands were closing around the boy's neck, Amanda reached into her purse and grabbed her gun, pointing it straight at Bryce.

"Get your hands off of him," she said with deadly calm, her finger steady on the trigger. She had always wondered what it would take to make her use the gun. Now she knew. "I said to let him go, dammit."

The order fell on deaf ears. She took one look into Pete's scared eyes, aimed the gun at Bryce's elbow, and fired, shattering the bone. He screamed in agony, releasing his hold just enough for Pete to get away.

"You okay?" Amanda asked Pete, not taking her eyes off the PI.

He rasped out something that sounded like a "yes."

"Go out to my car and call 911."

Pete shook his head. "Won't leave you," he croaked out, his expression belligerent.

Another stubborn male, Amanda thought with a sense of amused resignation. She nodded toward the door. "Guess we'll all go, then. You first, Bryce."

He didn't seem inclined to cooperate, but the gun provided sufficient encouragement. Fifteen minutes later the neighborhood was crawling with cops. A half hour after that Donelli appeared. He dragged Amanda into his arms and held her. She could feel the unsteady racing of his heart. It finally slowed to a more steady rhythm.

She glanced up at him. "Guess I finally found a way to get you to break the speed limit."

He managed a rueful smile. "Not exactly. Harrison was

kind enough to pave the way with a call to the Highway Patrol. I had an escort all the way. What the hell happened?"

"Before or after I shot Bryce?"

"She got him in the elbow," Pete said proudly, sidling up to join them.

Donelli regarded him in astonishment. "Where'd you come from?"

"Good question," Amanda said. "He appeared just in the nick of time."

Pete instantly looked miserable. "It's all my fault in the first place. This guy paid me to stage that stuff in the park. I got to thinking about it. Something didn't feel right. So I've been keeping an eye on things around here."

"You've had me under surveillance?" Amanda couldn't believe her ears.

"Well, somebody had to do something," he said impatiently. "Joe here had hired the wrong guy."

Donelli chuckled. "I guess I owe you one."

"Damn right," Pete said, his cocky attitude securely back in place. He regarded Donelli slyly. "I could use a place to hang out. I'm not all that keen on going back to that park, not after what happened to that lady."

"Then you really are a runaway," Amanda said.

Pete's expression faltered just a little. "Yeah. That much was true." He looked from her to Donelli and back. "So, what do you think? I can always make do on my own, but it would be kind of nice to sleep on a real bed again. I could help out with the planting and stuff."

Donelli looked decidedly uneasy. "I've barely convinced her to marry me."

Pete shrugged. "Seems to me a woman like her could use us both." He regarded Amanda hopefully. "What do you say?"

Amanda thought she was getting in way over her head. She also had a feeling she was going to love it. "We'll talk about it."

A grin split Pete's face. "All right!"

A matching grin spread across Donelli's. "Ditto," he said.

CHAPTER

One

*T*HE suicide of Mary Allison Watkins bumped world politics, the Braves' pennant race, and a local business scandal right off the front page of Atlanta's papers. For two days the headlines were as tawdry as any tabloid's in America. They were fueled by speculation about why a beautiful, successful assistant to Georgia's senior senator would suddenly decide to drive her brand-new Jaguar straight into a two-hundred-year-old oak tree at a speed sufficient to jam the front bumper all the way to the tailpipe.

Joe Donelli waved the most gruesome of the front-page photos under his new wife's nose. "Let this be a lesson to you, Amanda," he said. "The way you drive, you're destined to wind up wrapped around a tree just like this one day."

Amanda shoved the newspaper aside. "It was a clear day," she informed him. "She was out in the country, for heaven's sakes. Traffic was light. According to authorities, no one had tampered with any part of the car. There was no evidence she ever hit the brakes. There was no medical reason, no sign of a stroke or a seizure or a heart attack, no alcohol or drugs in her bloodstream."

She drew a deep breath for her summation. "Therefore—and I have this on the best law enforcement and medical authority willing to be quoted by the media— Mary Allison Watkins aimed at that tree. It was a suicide, Donelli. Not an accident. It's not the least bit relevant to the way I drive."

"Maybe not," he conceded grudgingly. "But every time you squeal out of the driveway, an image just like this one forms in my mind. Call me overly protective, but I'd really like this marriage to last at least long enough to celebrate out first anniversary. We have ten months to go."

Amanda refused to be drawn into a lengthy discussion of her driving skills. If Donelli had expected a wedding ceremony to change all her bad habits, they were in a for a long period of adjustment. She was having enough trouble remembering to put the cap back on the toothpaste. Given their disagreements over that, a conversation about her driving could send them straight to divorce court.

"Why do you suppose she did it?" she asked, hoping to send his vivid imagination off in another, more productive direction.

Donelli had once been a crackerjack homicide detective in a tough jurisdiction—Brooklyn. He now dabbled in private investigations, when he wasn't tending his fields of corn, Vidalia onions, and tomatoes. No one she knew was better at devising theories and assembling the evidence to back them up. That was precisely why she wanted him focusing on Mary Allison Watkins's motivations and not on what he perceived as Amanda's dangerous driving skills. Given a little time, he was sure to come up with a couple of convincing arguments to go along with that sickening newspaper photo. Then he'd have her driving twenty miles an hour under the limit like some timid little old lady.

She met his gaze across the breakfast table. She still wasn't quite used to facing all that brawn and intelligence over cornflakes. She had to admit, though, that she rather liked it after all. She figured that was a good sign. Given the rocky road of their courtship, she hadn't been convinced she'd make it past the second week.

"Why would a woman who had it all kill herself?" she mused aloud, casting a sly look in Donelli's direction. He didn't seem to be jumping at the bait. In fact, he shrugged with seeming indifference.

"Obviously her life wasn't as rosy as it appeared on the surface," he said.

"According to the paper, she whizzed through college on an academic scholarship and never slowed down. She had a responsible position with a powerful senator. She was intelligent and gorgeous. She was engaged to be married to Representative Zachary Downs, one of the most eligible bachelors on Capitol Hill and a rising star in the House." Amanda shook her head. "I just don't get it."

"Maybe she and Downs were having problems."

She waved off the possibility. "Have you seen the interviews he's done? The man is devastated."

"Amanda, would you really expect him to be doing cartwheels down Pennsylvania Avenue? If they were having problems, it's hardly something he'd be inclined to reveal under these circumstances. He'd keep it private."

"So you buy the suicide theory?"

"I haven't seen any evidence to the contrary," he responded cautiously as if he sensed that it was a trick question.

"Then how come no one has found a note?" she demanded, seizing on what she saw as a significant flaw in his argument—and everyone else's, for that matter.

"Why hasn't one single person come forward to talk about how depressed she was over something, *anything?*" she added. "To hear her friends talk about her, Mary Allison was more upbeat than one of those disgustingly cheery morning talk show hostesses. It was one of the traits that made her so successful in Washington. Nothing rattled her."

Donelli looked bemused. "Not five minutes ago you were telling me it was suicide. You laid out all the evidence, detail by detail. Let me guess. At that moment, it was a convenient explanation. Now you have another agenda."

"Not exactly. I'm just puzzled," she said as an idea began to take shape for an article for *Inside Atlanta*. "Did you see anything in the paper about the funeral?"

"If I had, I'm not so sure I'd tell you. Don't you think there's something a little bizarre about going to a stranger's funeral just to satisfy some morbid curiosity?"

"Morbid curiosity?" she repeated with what she hoped was convincing indignation. "I'm a reporter. I'm paid to be curious about things that don't add up. There's nothing morbid about it. Besides, who said anything about going?"

"I know you. I also know that you are a magazine re-

porter who is not assigned to do a story on Mary Allison Watkins. In my book, if you turn up at that church, that makes you no better than the voyeurs who watch those tabloid exposés on television."

Amanda ignored his disdain. She was more interested in his unconscious slip. "It was in the paper, then."

"I never said that."

"You mentioned 'that church' as if you'd read about where the service was going to be."

He shook his head. "Am I going to have to watch every single word I utter around you?"

"For all the days of your life," she assured him, reaching for the paper. That exasperating prospect ought to keep him from worrying excessively about whether she was off attending the funeral of a total stranger.

An hour later, however, she was careful to make the turn from the driveway onto the highway without squealing. It was important Donelli see that she could make some compromises in the name of marital harmony.

There were so many carnations, roses, gladioli, and other more exotic flowers at the front of the stately old Episcopal church that the air reeked with their heavy, sweet scent. With the pews filled to capacity and the overflow crowd jammed along the aisles, it was all Amanda could do to breathe.

Considering Donelli's low opinion of her presence at the funeral, she'd expected to feel like some sneaky tabloid reporter. Instead she was too busy trying to stir up a breeze with the little cardboard fan decorated with a picture of Jesus. His arms were held wide in a welcoming

gesture that relieved some of her guilt over being at the service.

"We are here today to mourn the loss of Mary Allison Watkins and to commend her soul to eternal peace," the minister intoned from the front of the church.

The mourners fell silent. Only a feminine sob, quickly muted, spoiled the solemn hush as the Reverend John Lawton repeated the Twenty-third Psalm. "The Lord is my Shepherd . . ."

Amanda let the soothing prayer flow over her as she surveyed the crowd. She spotted what had to be Mary Allison's family in the first pew—two women and a man. She couldn't guess the relationships, though there was a bit of a family resemblance between one of the women and the man. That same woman was flanked by Representative Zachary Downs and Senator Blaine Rawlings.

Even from a distance, the thirty-five-year-old Downs looked dry-eyed and stoic, his complexion ashen. Not once did his glance stray to the black-and-gold casket with its lavish blanket of white roses.

The distinguished white-haired senator had a supportive arm around the woman who, Amanda decided, must be Mary Allison's mother. She was obviously the source of those echoing sobs. Her thin shoulders shook with them. Periodically the senator bent close and murmured something, then offered her a pristine handkerchief, which she declined with a curt shake of her head. There was an anger to the gesture that was an odd counterpoint to the senator's seeming solicitousness.

Amanda wasn't sure what she'd expected to discover at the service, but she walked away from the church in the

pouring rain an hour later still feeling strangely disconcerted. The eulogies had been heartfelt and touching. The traditional hymns had been moving. But, like Mrs. Watkins's annoyance, something had been out of sync about the whole ceremony. She toyed with the possibilities all the way to the *Inside Atlanta* offices but couldn't put her finger on it.

It was past noon when she finally got to her desk, still puzzling over why Mary Allison's suicide bothered her so. Given the powerful people involved, the police investigation had been rapid and thorough. Publicly, at least, there hadn't been the faintest hint of doubt about the ruling that the young woman had taken her own life.

Yet try as she might, Amanda couldn't come up with a plausible explanation for a woman who'd shown absolutely no evidence of being distraught to willfully slam her car into a tree on a virtually deserted Georgia back road.

After grabbing up a handful of tangerine jelly beans, she wandered into the editor's office. Sometimes just sparring with Oscar Cates helped her to pin down her chaotic thoughts. His tendency to take the official stance allowed her to give full rein to her love of playing devil's advocate.

Oscar was looking even more slovenly than usual this morning. He'd apparently dressed in whatever had tumbled out of the dryer, a mussed pin-striped shirt, wash-and-wear khaki pants, and a tie that could have used a trip to the dry cleaner. He could spruce up amazingly well for special occasions, but work wasn't one of them, especially

with his watchdog wife out of town. She usually sent him out looking presentable, at least.

Oscar glanced up from his computer, glared at Amanda over his hated reading glasses, and waved her toward a chair.

"In a minute," he muttered.

Amanda wasn't terrific at waiting. She paced.

Distracted by her movements, he looked up and scowled. "I thought I told you to sit."

"I wasn't aware it was an order," she said, and dutifully sat. She figured she had to at least start their conversation with a cooperative attitude if she hoped to get him to go along with her still somewhat vague story idea. She gestured toward the computer. "Go on and finish. I'll wait."

He regarded her suspiciously. Obviously she'd overdone being agreeable.

"What are you after, Amanda?"

"I wanted to discuss a feature for the next issue with you."

"A feature?" he repeated doubtfully. "I thought you considered all features to be fluff, a waste of trees, et cetera, et cetera, ad nauseam."

He was right. Generally she did think features lacked substance, but then she and Oscar had rather divergent opinions about what constituted a feature. He wanted fluff about historic home tours and quilting circles. She wanted to do an in-depth profile of a woman who'd committed suicide. At least she thought that was the angle.

"Maybe I used the wrong term," she said. "I've spent the whole morning thinking about Mary Allison Watkins. I think there's a story there. What would make a woman

like her kill herself? I could even talk to some experts about depression, signs of suicidal tendencies."

She added the coup de grace, which was bound to appeal to Oscar's image of *Inside Atlanta*'s noble role in the community. "It would be a real public service piece, especially in these stressful times," she said.

His expression brightened, just as she'd expected. "Public service, huh? I like that. I'm glad you're finally thinking of all the good we can do, Amanda. It's our duty to make a contribution to the way of life in this town. Not every story has to be a major exposé."

Amanda couldn't argue with his good intentions, even though her personal approach to journalism tended toward shining glaring light into shadowy corners. As far as she was concerned, that did more public good than all the cheerful features about annual parades, dogwood festivals, and historic restoration projects combined.

"So it's okay for me to go ahead with this?" she said. "I can put everything else on the back burner?"

His gaze narrowed. "You'll still give me some copy on the wives of the Atlanta Braves players, right?"

Amanda figured it would require about ten minutes to dash off the sort of puff piece he was looking for to go with the photo spread for the October issue. How hard could it be to sum up the wives' view of World Series mania? She could already guess how impossible their husbands were to live with as baseball season came down to the wire. Personally Amanda couldn't imagine anything more boring to write or to read. Still, she managed to inject the expected note of enthusiasm into her voice. "Absolutely."

"You figure you'll have this suicide thing for the next issue, too?"

She nodded. "Can you hold back maybe four pages in the middle, plus room for a jump?"

"In other words, you want the cover," he said with a sigh of resignation. "Damn it, Amanda, you were at the news meeting. You know I've already got a big business story in that space. Jack Davis has been pulling it together for the past month. What am I supposed to tell him?"

She resisted pointing out that that was his problem as editor. "Give me twenty-four hours on this before you finalize the cover. If I come up with something, we'll negotiate."

He looked as if he wanted to refuse just on principle, but it wasn't in Oscar's nature to turn his back on the possibility of a story that would undoubtedly boost circulation. Mary Allison had been viewed as a heroine in Atlanta, a local girl who'd stormed Washington and brought it to heel. Her suicide was good copy. If a scandal was attached, so much the better.

"You think there's something more to this, don't you?" he inquired hopefully.

"Oscar, I don't know what to think," she said honestly.

"Twenty-four hours, then. Not a minute more. Agreed?"

She glanced at her watch pointedly. "Twelve forty-six Wednesday. I swear it."

Back at her desk, she jotted down a list of prospective sources, beginning with Mrs. Watkins, Representative Downs, Senator Rawlings, and the senator's administrative aide, Gregory Fine, a weasley little man with whom

Amanda had already had one too many run-ins. No doubt there were other friends and relatives who could give her insight into Mary Allison's state of mind in the days before her death. She'd get to them later.

With no time to waste, she cast aside her distaste for intruding on a private moment of grief and called the Watkins house.

"Mrs. Watkins is in no condition to speak to the media," the man who answered told Amanda in a tone that managed to straddle the fence between southern charm and outright rudeness. "I'm sure you understand."

Whether she did or she didn't apparently didn't matter. He hung up on her.

She could have called back and hoped for a more cooperative family friend or relative, but something about the man's tone suggested that there wasn't a chance in hell that a reporter was going to be allowed to speak to the bereaved mother. It was exactly the kind of attitude that stirred Amanda's journalistic suspicions. Anyone who knew her could have told the man that warning her away would only strengthen her determination. She'd just have to go out there, preferably after everyone had left.

In the meantime, she called her favorite homicide detective, Jim Harrison, the only man she knew who was perpetually more rumpled than Oscar.

"Gee, it's been weeks. To what do I owe this honor?" he inquired. "I didn't think you were chasing knifings in the ghetto and drive-by shootings yet. That's all I've got on my desk."

"Maybe there's something that ought to be there," she suggested casually.

"You know about a body stashed somewhere?"

He sounded more amused than fascinated. Amanda decided to up the stakes. "Actually the body's buried, but I think the clues are elsewhere," she said. She could practically hear his mind clicking.

"Stop with the riddles, Amanda," he said finally. "Just spit it out."

"I was just wondering how closely the police checked Mary Allison Watkins's car."

"I read the same papers you do. The experts went over that car with a fine-tooth comb."

"Looking for?"

"Mechanical malfunctions."

"What about paint from another car?"

Dead silence greeted the suggestion.

"Oh, Detective, are you there?"

"I'm here."

"Well?"

"You know it's not my case," he said predictably.

"But I do know you love to dabble in things mysterious. How about checking with the technicians who went over that car? Maybe finding out where it's stashed so I can go take a look at the paint myself?"

"You're opening a real can of worms here, you know that, don't you?"

"Not unless somebody's covering something up," she reminded him. "If everything's just as it's supposed to be, I'll have nothing to report, will I?"

He sighed heavily, something the men she knew tended to do a lot.

"You know I trust your instincts, but just this once I

hope there was a major glitch with your reception," he said.

"You'll check, though, won't you?"

"I'll check. I'll get back to you when I know anything."

Amanda read through the computer files on the accident one more time. By then it was nearly rush hour. She left the office and drove to the neighborhood of aging middle-class homes where Dee-Ann Watkins had raised her superachiever daughter. There were still a dozen or more cars in the driveway and lining the shaded street in front of the small brick ranch-style house. Amanda parked down the block and settled back to watch.

At seven o'clock the last of the mourners began to straggle out. A limo turned the corner, then double-parked in front until Zachary Downs emerged from the house. He lingered on the front steps for a few final moments with Mrs. Watkins. Whatever he was saying did not seem to be consoling her. She looked every bit as angry as she had for that one fleeting second back at the church.

As he walked to the limo, he was joined by a young woman who had exited the house right after him. She had a classic blond beauty, enhanced by her understated but obviously expensive black suit. Even though it was dusk, she work dark sunglasses. Amanda tried to read Zack Downs's expression as he helped the woman into the limo, but it was enigmatic. There was no way she could guess the exact nature of the relationship.

After the pair had left, only two cars remained in the driveway. Amanda assumed that one of them belonged to Mrs. Watkins. She debated waiting for the owner of the second car to leave, then decided that more than likely

whoever remained was a relative or friend staying on at the house. With less than a day left to convince Oscar that she had a cover story for the next edition of *Inside Atlanta,* she didn't have time to waste.

She rang the bell, then waited, rehearsing the speech she hoped would get her inside.

After a lengthy delay, Mrs. Watkins opened the door. Her narrow face was pale, her eyes red-rimmed, but the look she directed at Amanda was more weary than confrontative.

Amanda introduced herself. "I'm terribly sorry to bother you at a time like this."

Dee-Ann Watkins studied her suspiciously. "You another reporter? I've already told the rest of 'em I got nothing to say."

"I'm with *Inside Atlanta.* I really would like to speak to you about Mary Allison's death. I promise I won't take up much of your time."

Dark brown eyes clashed with hers. "How come you didn't call it suicide like everybody else?"

Simple courtesy had kept her from using the word, but Amanda sensed something in Mrs. Watkins's reaction that kept her from admitting that. "There are a few things about that that puzzle me," she said instead.

"Is that so?" Mrs. Watkins said. "Well, to tell you the truth, I'm puzzled by it, too."

"Couldn't we talk, then? Perhaps we can clarify a few things," Amanda said, sensing that Mrs. Watkins was just itching to set the record straight. She added what she hoped would be the convincing argument. "I want people to know what Mary Allison was really like."

Mrs. Watkins gave a curt, approving nod at that and stood aside to let Amanda enter. "I'll tell you about my girl all right. And I'll tell you why I know with every bone in my body that Mary Allison didn't kill herself. She just wouldn't have done it, especially not now."